Seeing Ceremony

A NOVEL
with RECIPES

MEERA EKKANATH KLEIN

Seeing Ceremony

A NOVEL
with RECIPES

MEERA EKKANATH KLEIN

HOMEBOUND PUBLICATIONS
Ensuring the Mainstream Isn't the Only Stream | *Since* 2011
WWW.HOMEBOUNDPUBLICATIONS.COM

All Rights Reserved
Published in 2020 by Homebound Publications
Cover & Interior Designed by Leslie M. Browning
Cover Photo by © Sofia Zhuravetc
Interior Illustration by © Komleva
Interior Illustration by © Boverkoffeined
ISBN 9781947003675
First Edition Trade Paperback

10 9 8 7 6 5 4 3 2 1

Homebound Publications is committed to ecological stewardship. We greatly value the natural environment and invest in environmental conservation.

Homebound Publications is committed to publishing works of quality and integrity. In that spirit, we are proud to offer this book to our readers; however, the story, the experiences, and the words are the author's alone.

DEDICATION

To the *Nilgiris* (Blue Mountains) of my childhood.

This book is dedicated to childhood homes or places where happy memories are created. I want my readers to feel a sense of homecoming when they enter the fictional world of Mahagiri, a place where they can put up their feet and stay awhile, perhaps with a cup of piping hot cardamom coffee.

Welcome to Mahagiri, and I hope you enjoy your stay.

To: Linda

Happy Reading

Meeru

Nov. 2022

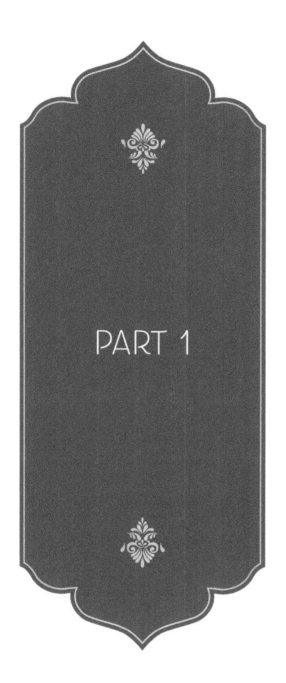

PART 1

CHAPTER 1
AT ODDS
(EARLY 1980s)

M‌Y MOTHER WAS ARRANGING MY MARRIAGE. AGAIN.

"A seeing ceremony is not the same as a wedding," she said in a firm voice. "You know, Meena, in ancient times a bride's family would hold a Swamyamvara to choose the groom."

"But we aren't living in ancient times, Amma," I said. "This is the twentieth century."

"I know, Meena, but a seeing ceremony is how it is done and I think it's a good way to find a suitable groom. I want you have an open mind about this." Her voice was very firm.

"I want to go to college, not get married," I shouted, knowing I sounded a bit petulant.

My mother's lips were a thin slash in her usually kind face. She glanced at our visitor before speaking to me.

"Meena, control yourself." Her voice was cold. "We have a guest here and she doesn't need to see you acting like a five-year-old. You are eighteen and a young woman."

Before I could help myself I blurted, "Then why do you treat me like a toddler?"

"Enough." My mother stood up and looked at the woman seated at our kitchen table. This was my old nemesis, matchmaker aunty. She was tall and skinny, a widow who favored white or pastel-colored saris. Her graying hair was twisted into a complicated knot on the back of her head and she had an annoying habit of snorting when she spoke. I looked down on the floor next to her chair and saw the inevitable cloth bag filled with bits of papers, notebooks and newspapers. Her bright eyes saw me looking at her bag.

"Ahh, Meena you remember my matchmaking bag?" she asked with a snort. "Everything you need for a good groom is in this bag." She picked up the bulging bag and placed it on her lap.

We called this noisy woman matchmaker aunty out of respect, not because she was related to us. I don't think I even knew her real name. She had been responsible for my first seeing ceremony nearly a year ago which had turned out to be a complete disaster when the groom failed to show up. I had refused to marry someone I had never even met. My entire family, including my mother, had been angry with me. I didn't think I could stand my mother's strong disappointment in me any longer and that is when I received an unexpected invitation from my uncle, my father's only brother who lived in California. His letter contained a student visa application and an invitation to get my undergraduate degree at the university where he was a professor.

"I will sponsor you," he had written. "I'll find a way to pay for your tuition if you can find money for the airfare to California."

I had shown the letter to my mother and she had seemed agreeable to my plans. We had talked about ways of raising money, maybe borrowing from the village money lender or asking a cousin for a loan. But now I was completely surprised by her insistence that I go through yet another seeing ceremony. The seeing ceremony was really an evaluation ceremony in my opinion. The groom or his family came to visit the prospective bride to "evaluate" her looks, her cooking skills and her home. I had felt like a horse or cow on display the last time I had gone through the ceremony. Perhaps this prospective groom would want to see my molars or check out my strong thigh muscles. When I mentioned this to my mother, she completely lost her temper.

"Meena, you are an extremely spoiled and selfish girl and not thinking about anyone but yourself."

When my mother lost her temper she didn't yell. Her face grew darker and her brown eyes flashed with temper and she spoke in a quiet, almost gentle tone.

"You will do as you are told," she continued. "I've had enough of your insolence."

"This would never happen if father were alive," I yelled. "He would have never forced me into a marriage."

My mother's stricken look told me I had gone too far. It had been barely three years since my father had died from a sudden heart attack and my mother had been devastated by his death. She had withdrawn from me as well as my twin sister and brother who had been only six years old at the time of our father's death. It had been shocking to watch my mother's thick black hair become streaked with gray. My mother had become an old woman and I had agreed to the first seeing ceremony in hopes of cheering her up. After the seeing ceremony ended in disaster, I thought we had come to some sort of understanding. I had actually hoped she would support my plans to go to America. But now it seemed she had her own plans for my future and had brought matchmaker aunty back into my life.

I ran out of the room, not caring if I was acting rude and childish.

CHAPTER 2
MY MOTHER

The Pandava brothers and their cousins the Kauravas were bitter rivals of the Kuru dynasty. Well, the story of Princess Draupadi takes place when Duryodhana Kaurava was crowned king. The five Pandava brothers shared a wife, a beautiful princess named Draupadi. Now, Duryodhana was always looking for ways to humiliate the Pandavas and knew that Yudhishthira the eldest Pandava brother had a weakness for gambling. He invited Yudhishthira and his brothers to a game of dice at his palace. His uncle Shakuni played with a pair of magical dice that allowed him to win, whatever the odds. As the night wore on poor Yudhishthira kept losing. He lost his horses, his chariots, his jewelry, his palace and even his brothers and himself in the game. Finally, only his wife, the princess Draupadi was left and Yudhishthira gambled her away too.

In their arrogance the Kauravas had the princess dragged into the court. She was declared public property and one of the evil Kaurava cousins, Dusshasana, pointed out that even her sari now belonged to them. That is when Dusshasana dragged Draupadi by her long hair into the center of the room, intending to tear off her sari. The princess wept and begged for someone to help her, but everyone turned away. Her husbands looked ashamed and Yudhishthira wept with humiliation and anger.

Dusshasana laughed at her frightened look and roughly seized the end of Draupadi's sari and attempted to disrobe her. At first Draupadi tried to hold onto her clothing and dignity but Dusshasana was too strong and she found herself being twirled

ɔelpless doll. Finally, she decided to call on a family
). This friend was none other than Lord Krishna, an
shnu. Then a miracle happened. Even as Dusshasana
eling and tugging, the sari seemed to grow and grow.
Sou... s and yards of material piled up next to Draupadi as
Dusshasana tried his best to strip away the fabric. He finally grew
weary and had to give up. Shakuni then grabbed the sari and began
to tug it off, but after a while he too had to admit defeat. One of the
elderly Kaurava uncles finally called a halt to this madness and to
the astonishment of the courtiers, Princess Draupadi left the room
with her honor intact."
—*The story of Princess Draupadi as told my Meena's mother*

My name is Meena, short for Meenaskhi, the goddess who has her own temple in a faraway city. My home is the hilltop town of Mahagiri in a large and lovely white-washed house with a red tile roof. At this time, our household consisted of my mother, my twin nine-year-old siblings Appu and Thangam, a family cousin we called Muthi or granny, and Devi, our housekeeper and cook. My mother had a thriving cow milking business and she employed several men from the neighboring village. Among them was Raman, a cowhand, who was married to our maid Kashi. They had a one-year-old baby boy named Mohan. Kashi's father Bhojan was one of my mother's most trusted cowhands and her business confidant.

If the heart of our bungalow was the kitchen, and then the soul of the house was my mother. She had been devastated by my father's unexpected death and she had never fully recovered from this loss. Even though she smiled and joked with us, there was always a hint of sadness in her eyes. She no longer wore the bright red bindi dot on her forehead; instead her forehead, which had more lines on it now, was adorned with the pale yellow marking made from sandalwood paste. After my father died, she had tried to wear white saris, to express her mourning, but this proved to be too impractical when working in the garden or milking the cows. She had given away her bright yellow and orange silk saris and now draped herself in more subdued colors. The muted blues, greens and grays somehow matched her somber mood and inner sorrow.

My father's death had been particularly hard on the twins. They had clung to me for months and I had to sleep with one or the other each night. But now that three years had passed the thoughts of my father mostly brought me happiness and we all spoke of him with affection and warmth. Sorrow was for the old.

I was subdued the next day and even though I wanted to apologize to my mother for my outburst I couldn't find the words or courage. With each passing moment it was getting too late to say sorry. So both of us pretended I had never yelled and we went about our day. We avoided each other and spoke only when it was necessary. Muthi and Devi tried to play peacekeepers.

"She's your mother," Muthi said in a soft voice. "She just wants the best for you."

"But what if she's wrong, Muthi?" I asked.

The older woman looked taken aback at my question. She fingered the large gold thoda earrings on her long ear lobes and shook her head.

"In my day, mothers always knew what was best."

I didn't bother arguing with her because I knew she would never change her opinion. Later that evening while the twins were taking a bath and before the evening prayers and meal, I decided to visit the quiet kitchen. I sighed to myself as I looked out the kitchen window. The sun was setting and the long shadows looked spooky among the eucalyptus trees that bordered our property. I turned away from the darkening trees and looked west. The hillside on this side of the house was covered in green tea bushes and the natural green carpet was bathed in golden light turning it into a magical kingdom. Soon the sun would disappear over the highest hill and darkness would fall on my home. I looked around the old room. It had seen better days but it still had a welcoming comforting presence. I could feel the love of many people who had worked hard in this room to prepare pilafs, curries, breads and sweets to feed us all these long years.

I heard a noise behind me and turned around to see Devi entering the kitchen to start preparing the evening meal.

"Devi," I called out.

She was startled at the sound of my voice but when she saw me, her face lit up with a huge smile.

"Kutty, what are you doing here in the dark?"

"Nothing," I said, moving away from the window. "I was just thinking how much I'm going to miss this kitchen."

Devi shook her head at me and turned on the kitchen lights. Yellow light bathed the familiar room. The walls were smoky, having absorbed the flavors and spices from thousands of meals. There were bunches of onions, herbs and garlic braids hanging from the rafters. Harvested potatoes, cabbages and a few carrots were stored in baskets beneath the table. The hearth which took up most of the space in the kitchen was used primarily for heating large pots of water. Nowadays Devi used the two gas burners to do most of the cooking. I sometimes missed the smell of wood smoke and frying onions. Somehow cooking on the gas stove didn't conjure up the same aromas. However, nothing remained the same and even I had changed over time. I had grown in the last couple of years. No longer skinny and shy, I had matured taking care of my mother when she was grieving for my father and there was a self-confident air about me.

"I wish I knew what to say to Amma," I said to Devi as I watched her chop onions and peppers. "I don't like being angry with her."

Devi wiped her streaming eyes on the end of her cotton sari. "I know, little one," she said. "You will have to find a way to apologize to her. She loves you and will listen to you."

I nodded, not quite convinced. "I know but I don't know what to," Devi interrupted me.

"Kutty," she said, even though she knew I hated to be called *child*, "Sometimes you have to step away to get the best look. Your mother loves you but you are her daughter and you are just as strong and independent as her. I know you will figure it all out."

Devi pulled me into her strong arms and I found comfort in her sturdy body. After a few minutes she pulled back and looked up at me.

"Both of you spoke in anger," she said. "You need to forgive her and then try to convince her about your plans."

"I don't know what to say" I sighed. "I need to talk to someone."

"How about your Scottish friend?"

"You mean Mac?"

Devi nodded, busy kneading whole wheat flour for our evening rotis. Of course Mac would have the answer. I've known Mac since I was a small child and he was the kindest man I'd ever known.

"Go talk to your friend and let me get on with making my lemon rasam and rice," she said. "I'll make it the way you like."

Devi's lemon rasam was a creamy blend of red or yellow lentils, garlic, hing and fresh lemon juice. It was tangy and soothing and delicious over freshly cooked Basmati rice and dipped into warm rotis.

I telephoned Mac and asked if I could visit him. He invited me to afternoon tea and we agreed to meet the next day. Making those plans made me feel a little better, more proactive and positive. That evening after dinner I once more ventured into the kitchen looking for my mother. This time of day had always been sacred to my mother who liked to use the quiet of the evening to unwind. When I was young, I had enjoyed being part of this nightly ritual, but for the past few years I usually came in just to say goodnight and sometimes to get a glass of water before going to my bedroom. During my high school years I had homework and sometimes sleepovers or time with friends. But tonight I was feeling sad and wanted to spend time with my mother and Devi and so I slipped into the warm kitchen. The fire had been banked down in the hearth, and all the burners on the gas stove were turned off.

Devi called out to me, "Come in, kutty, we were just about to have some turmeric milk. Would you like some?"

I nodded yes and locked the door leading to the front of the house before joining the two women. The kitchen was dim and Devi's shadow danced on the white washed walls. My mother was seated at her usual spot, right in front of the fireplace. She was leaning against the warm wall, her legs stretched out in front of her. I felt teary-eyed as I joined her on the straw mat.

"I'm sorry, Amma," I said leaning against her warm body.

She put an arm around me and hugged me close, 'Shh. It's alright, Meenakutty." she said, using a childhood endearment. "We both said things we didn't mean. I love you and want the best for you."

She pulled away so she could look at me, "Kutty, I grew up as an orphan and even though my aunty Seetha took care of me, I missed my mother and her love."

She was silent as she remembered her mother. I had heard the story about how her parents had tragically died when the bullock cart driver had fallen asleep and let the animals lead the cart into a muddy ditch. The driver had managed to jump out, but he couldn't get to her parents who were trapped under the overturned cart. The ditch was filled with the heavy monsoon rains and her parents' bloated bodies had been discovered the next day.

"Ever since then I promised myself that I would make sure my children were safe and had someone to take care of them. Then your father died...." Her words trailed off.

I leaned closer to her and she sighed and continued, "I am terrified that I too will die and you will be an orphan."

"I know, Amma," I said.

"Just go through this seeing ceremony for my sake, kutty," she pleaded with me. "I think you might be pleasantly surprised."

So against my better judgement, I agreed.

My voice was a little unsteady and I took a deep breath. "I just want everything to remain the same."

My mother put an arm around my shoulder and hugged me tight.

"Change is the only thing that is constant, my little one. If we didn't change and grow, we would all remain babies."

CHAPTER 3
MAC

THE STORY OF THE SELKIE
A SCOTTISH LEGEND

Once upon a time there was a fisherman who lived on the famous Pentland Firth in the North Highland County on the shores of the grey Atlantic Ocean. He earned enough to feed his family by fishing, crabbing and trapping lobsters. Now not far from where he caught lobsters and shellfish were large rocks that attracted huge groups of Selkies or seals. The fat creatures with their silken coats lay on the rocks sunning themselves. The fisherman wanted to catch one of these Selkies and sell its beautiful coat. He saw a huge bull seal with a beautiful pearly gray coat and decided to hunt the creature. He approached it cautiously, sliding on his belly, with his huge hunting knife in his hand. He was so quiet that he was almost upon the dozing seal before it caught scent of him and turned to flee but not before the fisherman slipped his knife into the seal's flesh. The seal gave out a terrible cry but managed to dive off into the ocean.

The fisherman left the shore, despondent about losing his hunting knife and the big Selkie. He was sitting by his hearth that evening when a stranger knocked on his door. The stranger, a bearded young man with big brown eyes, asked him if he was a Selkie hunter and when the fisherman replied he was, the young man said he had a buyer who was interested in proposing a business partnership with the fisherman. The young man insisted that the fisherman come with him and meet the businessman right away. The stranger was on a horse and asked the fisherman to climb behind him.

Instead of taking the fisherman to the village, the young man rode to the edge of the ocean. They dismounted and he asked the fisherman to look into the crashing waves. When the fisherman leaned over the side of the cliff, the young man pushed him into the cold sea. The man thought he would drown but by some miracle he found he could breathe underwater. He saw an open door ahead and he floated inside. He entered a huge hallway, lit with many candles, and filled with many Selkies. All of them were in mourning, some crying out loud and some weeping silently. The man looked at his reflection and was surprised to see he was a Selkie too. He didn't have much time to ponder this because the young man (who had turned into a Selkie) came up to him with a knife. Is this your knife, the young man asked? The fisherman said it was the knife he had used to kill a bull Selkie. That Selkie was the king of all Selkies, the young man said. The fisherman began to weep thinking the Selkies meant to kill him. He started to beg for his life but the young Selkie stopped him and said he needed the fisherman's help to heal the bull Selkie. He asked the fisherman to press the wound closed. When the fisherman did this, the wound closed and was healed by magic. There was great rejoicing in the hall. The fisherman was taken back to the surface by the young Selkie. The fisherman was relieved to be back in his human form. The young Selkie, who had turned into a young man, asked the fisherman to never hunt for Selkies. The fisherman promised and vowed to protect Selkies he saw on the sea shore. In gratitude, the young man gave the fisherman a bag of gold coins and rode off into the mists." —As retold by Mac.

The next day I decided to wear a lavender silk skirt and one of the purple and white sweaters my mother had knitted me for my afternoon tea with Mac. My hair was braided and I had a bright purple bindi dot on my forehead. Muthi had decided to accompany me so she could visit her old friend Mala, Mac's housekeeper. Muthi was dressed in immaculate white robes and her large gold thoda earrings gleamed and sparkled in the late afternoon sunlight.

It was a bright and beautiful afternoon so we decided to walk to Mac's house. We walked through the back door, past our vegetable garden. Tomato season was over but there was a fresh crop of potatoes waiting to be dug up. Even in late August, our garden was not dormant. There were rows of cabbage looking like over-sized green roses and a few feathery tops of carrots were visible above ground. On a workbench two varieties of spinach seedlings, waited to be transplanted.

At the corner of our property I climbed over the rock wall and helped Muthi over the rocks. We passed the tea stall where my old nanny Ayah liked to go for a cup of steaming hot tea and crispy road side snacks like deep- fried bread with gingery potatoes. Ayah had died a couple of years ago and I still missed her quiet wisdom.

I waved to Vasu who was busy making tea behind the wooden counter. Every time I saw him perform the ritual I was mesmerized. Even now I couldn't help pausing for a moment to watch him skillfully pour the reddish brown liquid back and forth between two large tin cups. He then poured the frothy milky tea into small tea glasses. Customers picked up the warm glasses and sipped the sweet tea with appreciative gulps.

"I guess there is no time for tea," I said to Muthi.

"Remember Mala is preparing tea for us."

I sighed and we continued our trek up the hill to a rocky path. This was the back way up the hill to Mac's mansion and estate. If we had been going by car, we would have had used the main road to his estate's impressive driveway and gates. Mac's tea estate was called "Highland Teas." Our cowhands Bhojan and Raman had nothing but praise for Mac.

"He is a fair and just man," Bhojan had said. "If I didn't work for your mother I would be on his payroll. He has helped so many of the villagers."

"How?" I asked, wanting to know.

"He buys tea directly from the laborers. For example, a village woman would pick green tea leaves on a plantation and instead of getting paid just for her labor; she would be paid for the amount of tea she picked. That way the plantation owner didn't have to pay for the labor and didn't have to use a middleman to sell his tea."

"The plantation owners who were part of the Highland Tea estates, which later was named Big Mountain Teas, would have a guarantee that their tea would be sold every time. So the laborers never had to worry about being out of work."

The path was steep and Muthi was huffing and panting.

"Perhaps we should have gone through the main road," I said, a little alarmed at her deep breathing.

"I'm alright, Meenakutty," she huffed. "I just need to rest here for a little bit."

"Here" was my favorite resting spot, a large flat rock that overlooked the valley. From my high perch I could make out the red roof tile of our house and Bhojan's village in the distance. The main road was a gray ribbon snaking down the hillside. There was a moving green and yellow dot on it. The evening bus was returning from Upper Mahagiri. The sun was starting a slow descent and the entire valley was bathed in a golden hue. Here with the cool evening air on my face and the glow of the setting sun, I could feel my father's presence. I couldn't explain the feeling but I felt blessed and at peace.

I thought back to when I had first met Mac. I must have been about three or four years old and had been playing in the fruit orchard with our maid Kashi. I had wanted to hide from her and I had quickly clamored up the old pear tree. Going up was easy. But when I looked down the ground seemed far away and suddenly I was frightened and started to cry and called out to Kashi to help me.

"There, there, what's all this fuss about?" a voice spoke just below me. I stopped weeping and peered down through the green leaves and into a pair of the bluest eyes I had ever seen. Well, I had never seen anyone with blue eyes and so they were my first and I forgot to be scared.

"Are you a giant?" I asked the man with the blue eyes, pale skin and thick white hair. He had a beard that was neatly trimmed and thick eye brows.

He gave a booming laugh and shook his mane of white hair, "Nay lass, I'm just a Scottish man on his morning walk and then I heard some crying and thought to meself that is surely a fairy caught in a fly web."

I smiled at his accent which sounded like his mouth was full of bread. "That was just me, not a fairy and I'm not in a web. I'm stuck in a tree."

"Nay lassie, you are just having a bit of fun," he said. "Come now, come on down."

"I don't know how," I wailed, suddenly afraid again.

"Why just the way you went up," the man with the blue eyes said. "Now look around you. You are sitting on a sturdy branch aren't you?"

"Yes."

"Well, look down and right where your left leg is dangling is another branch. Use your arms to swing down on that branch and try to step on it."

I took a deep breath and looked down. I could see my mother and Kashi standing beside the "giant" with anxious looks on their faces.

For the next few minutes I followed the man's instructions and calm voice until I was on the lowest branch.

"Jump down, lassie," he said. "You have made it."

I couldn't believe it; I was back on solid ground.

"Thank you," I said, running and hugging his legs.

"Yes, thank you so much," my mother spoke up "for helping my daughter come down from a place where she had no business going in the first place."

"Now, now, no harm, no foul eh? Girls should climb trees," the man said. He stuck out his right hand and said, "Name's Ian Andrew MacPherson. I live up the hill from your house. Highland Teas is the place."

"Of course," my mother said shaking his hand. "I'm Sudha and this little one is Meena."

"What do you say to Mr. MacPherson?"

'Thank you for helping me down Mr. Mac.MacPherson," I tried to say his name.

"Nothing to it but the name is Mac. Just Mac to everyone."

We had become firm friends after that first meeting. Mac became a frequent visitor to our house and advised my mother on growing crops, including some tea bushes, and she introduced him to south Indian food. I had spent a lot of time in his library, reading or playing checkers by the roaring fireplace. Over the years his quiet guidance had been valuable and now I was hoping he could help me once more.

"We'd better get up the hill," Muthi's voice brought me out of my reverie.

The sun was getting lower and the air was growing cooler as started our journey again. The hillside gave way to a curved path that led me down a slope and onto a beautifully manicured green lawn which lay below me like an emerald isle, a rectangle of peace.

The green was marred by several colorful items. As I got closer I could see they were bright colored balls, and what looked like wooden hammers. There were metal wickets stuck into the ground and I knew this was part of Mac's croquet set. He loved this game of croquet.

"Closest thing to golf these days," he used to say with a smile.

Since my last visit a few weeks ago, Mac had built a plastic covered building on one corner of the lawn. A bouncing ball of fur came flying down the path toward me.

"Hey Duffy, old boy." I kneeled down and petted the dog which was wagging its entire backside with excitement at seeing me.

"What kind of guard dog, are you? Will you lick a burglar to death?" I asked, scratching the dog's rounded belly.

I looked up to see a tall figure coming down the path. "Hey Mac," I called out.

"Ah, I see you have already been greeted by Duff. Meena, it's so good to see you. Have you grown another inch since I saw you last? When was that?'

"Not that long ago," I replied. "It's only been a few weeks."

He turned to Muthi, "So good to see you, Muthi."

He spoke in the local dialect and Muthi giggled at his accent.

"Is Mala here?" she asked.

"Yes, she is in the kitchen."

"I'll go help her. Meena, let me know when you are ready to go."

I nodded and watched her walk toward the house. I turned back to Mac, "How are you, Mac? It's good to see you too." I went over and hugged him, smelling his familiar scent of wood smoke and tobacco.

"How have you been?"

"No complaining lassie, just getting a bit older, that's all."

I nodded but couldn't help noticing that he was limping and leaning on his cane a bit more.

"Did you and Muthi hike up here?"

"We did and it was beautiful. I love the view from your hill. I could see my house and the village beyond that."

"It is a pretty place. At times it reminds me of another."

I was about to ask him what other place but he stopped in the middle of the path and turned to me, "Would you like to see the greenhouse."

"So that's what that building is. Did you just build it?" I asked.

With Duffy right at our heels we walked into the plastic covered building. It was very warm and snug in the greenhouse.

"Yes, it went up a few weeks ago and I've already started experimenting with different tea varieties," said Mac. Two long tables covered with small containers of green tea bushes.

"These are going to be grown without pesticides. Chemicals can't be good for people."

"My mother says the same thing and has started using less spray on her potatoes," I said.

"Your mother has always been ahead of her time. I should compare notes with her soon."

I admired the small pots of green herbs.

"Winter thyme and parsley and some chives," Mac pointed out.

Along with the herbs, there were flowers and even a lone banana plant.

We walked around and then Mac led me outside, "Come on, tea is waiting."

I followed Mac and Duffy out of the warm greenhouse and into the cool evening. The front yard was a profusion of dahlias, roses and daisies. It was as if the garden had gone wild. How would anyone know a weed from a flower in this glorious mess?

We passed the side yard of the bungalow and I couldn't help thinking how different it looked from the colorful messy one in front. Here the bushes were all equi-distant from one another. The walkways were precisely laid out and burnt-orange bricks lined the edges of the path. I paused a moment to admire a bush pruned to look like an elephant.

"You like that eh? That gardener sometimes gets carried away with his shears."

"It's lovely," I said.

We climbed the curved steps to the front door and as if by magic the door opened as we approached it. A little old lady smiled at me.

"Meena! How you've grown," she said with a huge grin. "You must be getting married soon."

I felt the smile melting off my face as Mala's question reminded me why I was here.

"My mother would like me to," I replied in a light tone.

But Mala wasn't done. "Are there any plans for your marriage? I heard the matchmaker was visiting the Big House."

The villagers called our house the Big House, even though it wasn't the biggest or fanciest house in the area. They all loved my mother and called her Little Mother because she was willing to help anyone in need. I guess they thought her big heart couldn't be contained in a little house so they called our modest cottage the Big House.

I quickly changed the subject, "Everyone is fine. You should come visit us sometime. My mother always asks about you."

"I will try. Give her my regards; right now I'm enjoying visiting with Muthi."

Mac took charge, "Miss Mala, please bring tea and scones to the library for us."

I was glad to leave the inquisitive Miss Mala and follow Mac into his library which happened to be my favorite room. As always I was taken aback by the number of books in this wood paneled room. Every wall was covered with book shelves. The one wall without books was taken up by a large stone fireplace where a huge fire was burning merrily. I could hear it snapping and crackling from the doorway.

"Come on in, Meena," said Mac, as he made his way to his favorite chair by the fire.

I walked into the room, the warmth from the fire enveloping me. The fire was welcoming even though it wasn't winter yet, the stone house was always damp and cold. I glanced up at the huge trophy of a large fish mounted on a board above the fireplace. As a child I had loved to play with all the clocks on the mantel piece. I took a seat on one of the chairs facing the fire. There was a long leather sofa and matching love seat on the other side of the room.

Mac sat down and pulled out his pipe and started fiddling with it. When he finally got it started he took a long puff and let out a sigh.

"I always forget how many books you have," I said with a laugh.

He nodded. "I think that was the main reason I didn't leave India when the rest of the chaps returned to Scotland and England. How was I going to lug all these books across the ocean? Besides, Mahagiri is my home."

"Do you miss Scotland?" I asked.

"I do at times. I was born in the Highlands and every once in a while I crave the cool breezes, the smell of the moor and burr of the Scottish tongue. But then Miss Mala comes in with a plate of biryani or tikki masala and I soon forget my Scottish dreams." He laughed his booming laugh.

I couldn't help smiling. I looked at the man across from me. Most days I almost forgot he was a foreigner with pale skin and blue eyes. He was just Mac. As a teenager I heard his story and found it impossibly romantic. It was Miss Mala who told me Mac's story.

"The master's name is Ian Andrew MacPherson and he was born in the Highlands of Scotland. From what I have heard from the master, life in the Highlands was harsh. The weather was always cold and he lived in a large drafty house made of stone blocks. His family owned some land. He had a good education but as the second son he knew he would inherit nothing from his parents. In those days second sons were asked to join the military or go into church service.

"Master always said he was too restless to settle into some parish as a priest. He loved horses and joined an army called Royal Scots Greys. Now the Royal Scots Greys were part of an old cavalry regiment of the British Army known as the Royal Scots Dragoon Guards. They were also known as the Grey Dragoons because they rode grey horses. After several name changes that I can never keep track of, the Royal Scots Greys was formed. The master joined the regiment and was sent to Libya and Lebanon and eventually made his way to the north of India. He was stationed in Kashmir sometime before the partition."

Miss Mala had leaned forward, her eyes glistening with excitement, "This is where the story gets interesting.

"The princely state of Kashmir was ruled by Ranbir Singh. One of his many cousins lived in the palace and one cousin had a beautiful daughter by the name of Narmin. Narmin means soft and delicate like a flower.

"This Narmin was not soft and delicate. She was outspoken and headstrong and did not listen to her father or mother. She loved riding her horse on the meadows and going far from the villages and small cities. One day when she was out in a meadow, the weather took a turn for the worse and suddenly the skies opened up and rain began to fall in hard sheets. Afraid that her horse would hurt itself and she would be thrown, Narmin looked for some place to wait out the storm. She saw a goatherd's shed in the valley below and thought she could rest there until the storm passed. She jumped off her horse and led the animal to the overhang by the small mud building. There was a short wooden stake, so she tied her horse and stepped inside the crude building.

"She was relieved to see that the building was empty. It was a depressing place, with walls made of crumbling mud bricks and a dirt floor, but it was dry. The only light was coming from a small opening in the back wall. There was a broken bed frame in one corner and Narmin perched on one end, hoping the storm wouldn't last too long. She had wrapped a delicate shawl around her shoulders and was leaning against the mud wall, almost asleep, when the wooden door, which had been standing ajar, was pushed aside violently. She sat up in alarm and saw two young men enter the room. They were busy talking to each other and didn't notice Narmin sitting in the corner. When they finally did, they both stopped talking and stared at her.

"Now Narmin was very beautiful and even with her hair hanging around her face in tangles and all her makeup washed off by the rain, she was breathtaking. To the two men, who happened to be farm laborers, she must have looked like a heavenly vision.

"One of them came up to her and asked her what she was doing. Narmin stood up, tossed the end of the silk shawl over her shoulder and told them to leave the hut immediately. That is when one of the young men noticed her gold chains, bangles and beautiful rings.

"Now as royalty, Narmin was always dressed in her best, even when riding by herself on the meadows. The men thought it would be easy to rob the young woman. So they asked her to hand over her jewelry. Of course Narmin being head strong and proud flatly denied them anything. In fact, she told them if they didn't leave, they would be sorry and her father's soldiers would cut them to pieces. The men laughed and decided to take the jewelry for themselves. They pushed the girl into a corner and while one of the men held her down, the other was about to rip off her gold chains when the wooden door was once again thrown open. A gust of cool air blew in and another stranger entered the old building.

"This was also a man but he was a foreigner with a ginger colored moustache and blue eyes. The young laborers thinking they outnumbered the foreigner attacked him. But the foreigner, for it was Mac, was a trained soldier and in a few moments had both men cowering and cornered. He turned to Narmin and asked if he should kill the men. But Narmin who did not care for foreigners, even when they rescued her, said no. I will curse them instead; she said looking down at the cowering men. The men whimpered and begged her to spare them but Narmin ignored their pleas and said with great drama and flourish that their manhood would shrivel and wither away. Unless, she added, they honored all women from now on. Both men nodded and agreed. They fled into the rain as soon as the foreigner let them go.

"He then turned to Narmin and offered her his coat, which was quite wet and soggy. Narmin accepted and asked him to escort her to the nearest village. From there, she said, she could get an escort to the palace. Mac was bemused to learn that the beautiful maiden he rescued was a princess.

"Mac escorted Narmin home and her father was very grateful to him. But his gratitude turned to displeasure when Narmin and Mac fell in love. The lovers knew their union would never be blessed and decided to elope one night. But soldiers found them and in the fight, Narmin was fatally wounded. She died in Mac's arms. With her death, Mac was a changed and bitter man. He left the regiment and wandered all over India. His travels brought him to Mahagiri and he finally found peace here.

"He has been living here for a long time," Miss Mala had concluded her narration.

It was hard for me to imagine Mac as a young romantic man for there was a sturdy, almost granite-like quality about him. He was a man you could trust and I did trust him.

Mac sat back in his chair, "So tell me, Meena." He was interrupted by a knock on the door.

"Tea, Master Mac," Mala came in tottering a little under the weight of a huge silver tray. She placed the tray on the wooden table and looked at Mac.

"Shall I pour?"

"No, no. The lassie can pour. You go sit down a spell and visit with your friend."

"Ariight then," Mala said with a grin. I could never get over the strangeness of hearing her speak with a distinct Scottish burr.

"You sound so Scottish , Miss Mala," I said to her.

She laughed and gestured with her chin toward Mac. "You can blame him for my accent, Meena. You can't get away from that Scottish accent around here." Mala smiled down at their guest.

"I'm making my favorite sandwich for you to take back home. They are filled with spicy cilantro pesto and thin slices of boiled beets and potatoes. I'll send some along with Muthi."

I had never heard of such a combination.

"I can't wait to try them, Miss Mala. Thank you."

I poured the amber liquid into the thick mugs Mac favored. There were no delicate bone China cups here. I handed him a cup of plain tea and added a drop of cold milk and a spoonful of sugar in mine. I took a sip of the fragrant tea.

"Ahh, Scottish tea," I murmured. "The flavor is so very different from Mahagiri tea."

Mac nodded, dabbing his lips with a cloth napkin. "This is one of the new varieties I was telling you about, a little different from actual Scottish tea. It's grown without pesticides."

He pointed at the silver tray, where a plate was filled with round scones.

"Help yourself to a ginger scone. They are Miss Mala's specialty."

I leaned forward and picked up a small round scone. The outside was shiny and dusted with sugar crystals that glistened in the firelight. My first bite was buttery filled with gingery flavor. There were bits of crystallized ginger as well as freshly grated ginger.

"This is delicious," I said.

I sipped on the smoky tea and felt myself relax in Mac's company.

"So, Meena," Mac said, "Your mother is arranging your marriage?"

I nodded and swallowed the last bit of scone, "Well, you know ever since my father passed away, she has been trying to arrange my marriage. She feels I need to be settled down before she dies."

"I can understand that," Mac said. "I take it you are not happy with this?"

"Nearly six months ago, she had me go through a seeing ceremony and it was a complete disaster. The groom never showed up and his aunt insisted I give her an answer right away on whether I wanted to marry her nephew or not."

"You said no?"

I looked up at his face and didn't miss the twinkle in his eye.

"It's not funny," I said a little huffily.

"I'm not laughing at you, Meena but I can imagine what the aunt said when you said no."

I laughed at the memory, although at the time it hadn't seemed so funny.

"Well, she was not happy. My mother was not happy either and it seemed like everyone in our family was angry with me."

I stopped talking and thought about that day when the matchmaker and the groom's aunt kept insisting that I say yes and how I had refused. Later an emergency family meeting had been called and one of my uncles, a retired school teacher, had pleaded with me to just say yes. But I couldn't and everyone in the room had yelled at me and the only thing that saved me was a letter from my uncle in California, inviting me to come attend college.

"It took over six months but I thought I had finally convinced my mother to let me go to California," I told Mac. "I thought she had come around to the idea, but just a few days ago she had the matchmaker over and was making plans for me to go through another seeing ceremony."

Mac put down his tea cup and leaned back in his chair. "What do you want to do, Meena?"

"I just want to go to college. I want to figure out where I fit in this world. Is that too much to ask?"

Mac shook his head and smiled at me. "Not at all. What you need is a way to present it that will make it acceptable for your mother.

"Meena, I'm just thinking out loud here but what is happening with your father's estate?"

"My father's estate?" I repeated his question as I realized I hadn't thought about my father's plantation since his death. He had owned a spice plantation in the village of Chandur, about hundred kilometers from Mahagiri. There on the hillside they grew cardamom, cashews, black pepper and some coffee and vanilla pods. His estate dried and processed the cardamom but my father had always sold the cashews and other spices to several merchants in nearby cities. He had made a good living and had about fifty laborers working for him. Most of them lived on his land and paid a small monthly rent for simple housing. The plantation was now run by my father's old manager, a good man named Murthy who had been with my father ever since he purchased the land.

"I hadn't thought about it," I confessed. "We still receive monthly reports from Murthy and we were all thinking everything is going well."

"Well, then, how about using the plantation to get some money to help you with your college expenses?"

"How?"

"Just bear with me here, Meena, I just had an idea. A good friend of mine is looking into investing in a spice plantation. He has an idea that a spice plantation will be a great place to start a co-op."

"What's a co-op?" I couldn't help interrupting Mac.

"A co-op is a way for farmers to get together and sell

their produce. My investor friend would like to get some spice plantation owners and start one. His plan is to protect the plantations and workers and eventually have the laborers buy into the co-op so they would get a small percentage of the profits when the co-op becomes profitable."

"It sounds great; something my father would have loved."

Mac nodded, "I agree. We need to convince your mom that this would be a good thing and if everything goes as planned, perhaps we can go on a trip together."

In theory Mac's idea sounded great but I was reluctant to think about selling my father's estate.

"But that would mean my father's estate will no longer be in the family," I said.

I couldn't explain my feelings to Mac. I had visited the plantation with my father about six years ago. I remembered the scent of the cardamom pods, pungent and sweet. The pepper trees were skinny and tall and yielded a fiery pepper that was a regional specialty. On that same visit, I had hiked to the top of a nearby hill and looked down at a breath-taking view. The valley, verdant and lush, was spread out in front of me. The air was thick and heavy with the scent of herbs and growing things. Everything around me was growing and flourishing like my father's spice plantation. The farm was a fertile place of hope and renewal and it was my father's legacy to me and the people who toiled on his farm. Was I ready to give all this up?

Mac was watching me with sympathetic eyes. He could see the play of emotions on my face.

He cleared his throat, "The idea is not to give up on your father's legacy but to build on it. My friend will consult with your family and be respectful of your father's wishes for the place but I think a co-op is a way to keep that way of life. Think on it, Meena. And an added bonus is that with the sale of your farm will give you some independence."

Even though I was filled with doubt, I decided I had no other choice. My mother would probably never give up trying to marry me off and if we had some cash, perhaps I could convince her to let me go to California. My mother was worried about money and didn't want to depend on my uncle for all the expenses. I just had to convince her.

"I'll have to think about this, Mac and after I convince myself, perhaps I can convince my mother."

"I can be there whenever you want and we can plan our trip."

I agreed to call him soon and I felt a tiny bit better about my situation.

"You aren't going to walk in the dark, are you?"

It was Mala. "Ramji can take you, kutty. Muthi has some sandwiches for you and your mother."

Muthi appeared in the doorway holding a package wrappednewspaper.

"Here are my famous beet and potato sandwiches with spicy cilantro pesto," Mala replied with a chuckle. "I'm sure you'll enjoy them. The sweetness of the beet is a harmonious accompaniment to the spicy cilantro paste and the sharp tang of lemon juice, grated ginger and green chilies all make this a delicious sandwich."

"I'm sure my mother will love them," I said. "She will want to see you to thank you in person."

"Perhaps next market day I'll stop by," Mala said.

When we arrived home I learned that my mother had gone to the local temple with the twins.

"There is a free concert tonight at the temple," Devi told me. "She has made some stew for you."

I thanked Devi and took my bowl of late-harvest stew to the dining room. Late harvest stew was a dish we usually had on cool foggy nights. It was a family favorite. My mother picked the late summer tomatoes, shriveled and almost dried up, from the vine. The tomatoes didn't look like much but they had a deep flavor that was rich and robust. First, my mother made a broth from tomatoes, lentils, onions and garlic.

Then she strained the flavorful broth and added bits of fresh vegetables. Tonight's soup had potatoes, carrots and long strands of fresh cabbage. This tangy stew also had fresh beans and the chunks of yellow squash. My mother enhanced the flavor of the broth with shavings of fresh ginger and a spoonful of coconut oil. Along with the stew my mother served whole wheat bread, chewy and piping hot.

I chewed on the bread and thought about my visit with Mac. I hoped my mother would listen to our idea for father's estate.

CHAPTER 4
SEEING CEREMONY

AN EXPLANATION

Arranging a marriage between a young man and a woman is a common practice in India. In an arranged marriage, the elders choose the life partner, but that was not always the case.

In Vedic times, royal families held a Swayamvara, a ceremony whereby suitable grooms from all over the country were invited. The bride was allowed to choose her own husband. Sometimes a contest of skill or strength was held and the winner won the bride. Even among non-royal families, young women were allowed to choose their own grooms or at least have a say in the matter.

But over the centuries, the rules of marriage changed and evolved. In modern India, many brides have no say in who they marry. In a recent survey conducted by Taj Group of Hotels nearly 85 percent of Indians, young and old, still prefer arranged marriages.

The elders, including parents of both the bride and groom, use a matchmaker to find the best match. Criteria such as religion, caste, culture, horoscope, profession and physical attributes are taken into consideration. If all or most of these criteria are met, the groom's family visits the bride to see girl and finalize the wedding plans. This is the "seeing ceremony."

—As explained by Sudha, Meena's mother

I woke up after a restless night and wandered into the kitchen, rubbing the sleep from my eyes. I was eager to talk to my mother but as always, mornings in her kitchen was a busy time. The cats were vying for a drop of milk while the cowhands, Bhojan and Raman, were trying to measure the fresh milk into large tin cans. Kashi was also there helping rinse buckets and strain the milk. This was not the time to have a heart to heart with my mother. Instead I turned to Muthi who was at her usual morning place, behind the large wooden table.

"You look like you need a cup of coffee," she said, handing me a steaming cup.

Gratefully, I gulped the hot drink. It was a perfect cup of coffee, strong, smooth, milky, slightly sweet and just hot enough.

I had grown up watching my mother, and later, Muthi make coffee in our kitchen. There was a certain rhythm and ceremony to the process. Muthi laid out all her necessary equipment on the wooden table. This included numerous cups, small steel containers, spoons, a jar of brown jaggery sugar and a tin can of freshly ground coffee. While the cowhands, my mother and Devi were busy with the milking, Muthi presided over her coffee table. Each cup was individually prepared. For Thangam and Appu, she would add just a tiny bit of freshly dripped coffee into a steel cup with handles, and then she would fill the cup with hot milk. Next she would add a generous spoonful of brown sugar and using another cup with handles, she would pour the milky liquid back and forth. When the drink was frothy and just the right temperature, she would pour it into a smaller cup for each twin. They would always have a wide milky grin after the first sip. Over the years, more coffee had been added to my cup and now I was sipping a strong and soothing drink that made me smile happily at Muthi. This was an additive brew, blended with fresh milk and just the right amount of affection. No coffee shop drink ever tasted this delicious.

I wiped the froth off my lips and put down the cup.

"There is nothing like your coffee to start the morning, Muthi."

"Meena." My mother placed a gentle hand on my shoulder.

"Amma," I stood up. "I'm sorry about last night. I didn't mean to yell at you."

She sighed, "I know, Meena. Once words are spoken, they can't be unspoken. We need to talk."

I nodded, "Alright."

"Well, finish your breakfast and come find me in the garden."

I tried to swallow the cracked wheat pilaf and banana raita, but the tiny kernels kept sticking in my throat. I took a gulp of my now-cold coffee. I usually loved the pilaf or Uppma which was full of flavorful pieces of fresh vegetables, ginger, sunflower seeds and nutty ghee. Devi served the pilaf with banana raita and the tangy mildly sweet sauce was a perfect accompaniment to the grains. I finally gave up on eating and left the half-finished plate on the kitchen table.

Would my mother agree to Mac's plan to sell my father's estate?

I walked outside past the stone wall and bathhouse to find my mother in the back garden. It was a cool morning and the tomato vines looked old and tired, a few stubborn red globes still clinging to the dying vines.

My mother was talking to one of our day laborers, "Time for the tomato plants to come out. Let's try to harvest all the green beans today."

She ended her conversation when she saw me. "We'll discuss what to do with the corner field later."

"Come with me, Meena," she said.

We made our way to a wooden bench. I can't remember when the wooden bench had been placed in the middle of the cabbage patch but the weather-beaten piece of furniture had become a popular gathering spot. So much so that someone had pulled up a couple of old logs and a large flat rock so it had the feel of a meeting place. It was the ultimate outdoor conference room, airy and bright. I sat on the bench and turned slightly so I was facing my mother.

"So," we both started at the same time. I stopped and we laughed.

"You go first, Amma," I said.

My mother looked down at her hands, avoiding my eyes.

"Well, matchmaker aunty has come up with a great match," she began.

"Amma," I interrupted her. "I thought we were going to talk about this."

She shook her head and looked up at me. "No, Meena. I think the time for talking is over. I asked you to come out here this morning to discuss the details of the seeing ceremony."

"This is my life you are talking about, Amma. Not buying a sari or cow."

"Watch your tone, Meena. As I was saying matchmaker aunty has a proposal and the groom is coming tomorrow evening to see you. No arguments."

I was so shocked that for a moment I forgot to breathe. Finally a burst of air escaped my lips and my lungs began to work again. I took a deep breath. Now was the time to tell her about Mac and my ideas for father's plantation.

"Amma, I will go through the seeing ceremony but you need to listen to what I have to say."

I hesitated. Not knowing how she was going to react.

She, too, took a deep breath. And I realized she was not keen on confronting me either. This gave me some courage to continue to speak

"I visited with Mac yesterday and he has found a really good investor to buy Achan's estate."

"What?"

The change of subject put her off kilter.

"What are you saying, Meena?"

"Amma, we have been allowing Murthy to take care of our spice plantation and it has worked so far but I think it's time to think about the future."

"And this future means getting rid of your father's legacy?" She sounded angry now.

"Not at all, Amma. The man who wants to buy the property has some great plans for the plantation to keep it going for decades. It will be exactly what Achan would have wanted."

"How do you know what your father would have wanted?" She sounded bitter and sad.

"You are right, Amma. I don't know but I do know he would want to protect the land and make sure his workers are taken care of."

My mother didn't say anything for a long moment. When she finally looked into my eyes she had tears in hers.

"You are right, Meenakutty. We have to think of your father's legacy. Tell me what Mac wants to do."

I explained about the co-op and the idea of selling the property to Mac's investor friend.

"The money will be something you can use for our future," I added.

My mother smiled and I was reminded of how beautiful she looked when she was happy.

"I don't suppose it would go into an education fund?" she asked in a teasing manner.

"I was thinking that," I admitted.

"Alright, Meena. Let's have Mac over for dinner in the next few days and we can talk. Meanwhile I need you to get ready for tomorrow's event."

Apparently there was no way to get out of the seeing ceremony.

Time always seemed to speed up when an unpleasant task was looming ahead. Now it flew by and soon it was the morning of the seeing ceremony. I had hoped the day would be gloomy and gray to match my mood. But it was a beautiful clear Mahagiri day and the blue skies and bright sunshine did nothing to cheer me up. Muthi made sure I used mung bean paste and fresh turmeric on my face and arms and legs. I had to admit the mixture did smell refreshing and pleasant. She helped me wash my hair which now hung below my waist. She patiently dried it and applied sweet coconut oil.

"When your hair is dry we'll braid it," she said. "Jaibal has brought some fresh jasmine flowers."

Jaibal owned a taxi cab and on occasions when our family needed a car, we always relied on him. We had known Jaibal for a long time and he had come into our lives in the most unusual way. When we were teenagers, my best friend Kumari Sen and I had caught a thief sneaking into our kitchen. The young orphan was just looking for a meal and my mother sort of adopted him and sent him to school. The boy, Jaibal, grew up and turned out to have an aptitude for fixing motors. He bought an old car and fixed it up and was now the proud owner of a taxi cab company in Greater Mahagiri.

In our bedroom, my mother had laid out a rich silk sari, the color of the Mahagiri sky, with plenty of gold threads. The sari reminded me of Mac's eyes and I hoped this was a sign that everything would turn out all right in the end.

So it was with a light heart that I allowed my mother to help me drape the sari. I gamely put on gold earrings and several gold chains, including a fancy intricate choker, along with several thin gold bangles. Next, she outlined my eyes with dark kohl and placed a large red bindi dot on my forehead.

"You look so beautiful," my sister Thangam said.

I smiled at her. "If you want you can help by bringing my gold sandals from the front room."

"Alright." She ran off happily.

My hair was now dry and Muthi braided it into one thick plait and entwined it with a long garland of fresh jasmine blooms. The sweet fragrance filled the room.

"Just see how you look, Meena." My mother led me to the large mirror on her dresser. "You are the most beautiful bride to be."

"Shh! Don't attract any evil eyes," Muthi warned, making a gesture to ward off evil spirits.

Matchmaker aunty bustled in, wearing an orange rayon sari brighter than her usual pastel-colored ones.

"Ah," she said looking at me. "She is good looking." Matchmaker aunty snorted and turned away from me.

"Little Mother, time for you to come to the front and be ready to greet the guests."

My mother patted me on the shoulder and left me. I carefully sat back down.

"Here, they are," said Thangam, who was back with the shoes. "The groom's car is here."

I let my sister help me with my sandals and then stood up to look out the bedroom window. But this bedroom faced the side yard and I couldn't see anything except a view of the jasmine vines. So I went back to sitting on the bed. Muthi had left to help Devi in the kitchen. Thangam sat down beside me.

"Are you happy to be married, Chechi?" she asked.

I looked down at her. Her big brown eyes were round and sparkling. I placed an arm around her shoulders and hugged her to me.

"I'm not sure if I'm happy or not," I said. "Ask me that after we meet the groom."

She giggled and then jumped up.

"I forgot to tell Muthi something."

She rushed off, leaving me alone in the bedroom. Restless, I got up and looked at my reflection in the mirror. It was like looking at a stranger. The make-up, the sari and the jewelry were not the real me. The real me, deep inside, was dressed in comfortable jeans and a cotton shirt with running shoes. That person wanted to be on a plane, traveling to faraway places, meeting new people. That person wanted....

My thoughts were interrupted by matchmaker aunty's loud voice.

"Stop daydreaming, Meena! I've been calling your name for the last few minutes," she said with her familiar snort. "It is time to meet your future husband."

She pulled me along then paused at the doorway, "Meena, just keep an open mind about this groom. He's a doctor and well connected."

"What do you mean?" I asked, imagining the worst.

She patted my arm and shifted the wad of tobacco in her mouth from one side to the other. "Just be open-minded." She snorted again.

Now I was really alarmed and wanted to go back to the safety of my bedroom but there was no escape. My mother was at my side now and was gently but firmly propelling me into the living room.

I entered the familiar room feeling like a stranger in my own home. How many times had I come into this comfy room, ready to jump on the sofa or find a seat on one of the wooden chairs? Like a modest bride, I kept my eyes on the ground, not because I was feeling traditional but because I was suddenly frightened to look up. Who would I see?

"Come, come, dear. Don't be shy," said a voice from the corner sofa.

My mother led me to the wooden sofa, guiding me to the voice.

I still couldn't bear to look up at who was speaking to me but from the corner of my eyes I could see her lap, a lap covered by a green silk sari. So this must be the mother or some other relative of the groom.

"Let me look at you," she said.

I felt fingers lifting my chin and I was looking into a pair of brown eyes set in a calm face that was plain, but not unattractive. She looked to be much older than my mother with gray hair pulled back in a tight bun. She wore no bindi mark on her forehead. A widow but dressed in a silk sari with a heavy gold chain around her neck. The bangles on her right hand jingled as she turned my face toward her.

"You are a beauty," she said and I could smell her breath, pungent with betel nuts.

"You will be perfect for my son. Go on, you can look at him." I wanted to tell her it was a little hard to turn and look when she had her fingers on my chin. She must have realized this and released my chin and pushed me. I got my first glimpse of my future husband. If this had been a movie, the music would have reached a crescendo. It would have perhaps been a bit ominous and foreboding. And then it would have screeched to silence because I could not believe my eyes. The man seated in the chair by the window was impossibly old and gray. I had to admit he was impeccably dressed in an expensive gray suit with a silk red and blue tie. His thinning hair was combed carefully back from his forehead and beneath his bushy eyebrows, he had the same intelligent eyes as the woman beside me. Was she really his mother?

Perhaps I looked as horrified as I felt because matchmaker aunty jumped in.

"She is a breathless beauty, isn't she, Doctor (snort)?"

The man held my eyes for a long moment and for the briefest second I could see a flash of sympathy, perhaps it was even pity. But before I could figure it all out, his eyelids closed and when he opened his eyes again there was no expression in them. Perhaps I had imagined the expression of sympathy.

"Wait," said my mother.

Suddenly she was at my side, pulling me up by my arm.

"This was a mistake. Please excuse us. Come, Meena."

I was bewildered but allowed my mother to tug me out of the room. I couldn't stop her anyway because she had a firm grip on my elbow.

"Amma?" I asked. "What is going on?"

But she kept pulling me and before I knew it we were out of the living room. But my mother didn't stop. We hurried through the dining room and it was only when we entered our kitchen that she finally released my arm. She didn't say a word. She just pulled me into her arms and hugged me close. I could feel her body shaking against mine. Was she having a fit? We had had a maid servant who was prone to epileptic fits and someone had to hug her tightly to keep her from thrashing around. I was now worried that my mother was also having a fit. I began to feel seriously alarmed.

"Amma? Are you all right?" I asked, a little breathlessly as she was still hugging me quite tightly.

But my mother said nothing—she just kept holding me. After a few minutes she finally released me and pulled away. I saw her cheeks were wet with tears. My mother was crying. She never cried. Now I was scared. "Amma, what is the matter?"

"Meena, forgive me. I had no idea about all this."

She was about to say more when the matchmaker stormed into the kitchen. Her chest was heaving and her face was red with suppressed anger.

"You," she said, pointing a dirty fingernail at my mother. "You are completely done. You think just because people in this small village call you Little Mother, you are someone special? I am done with you."

My mother released my shoulders and turned toward the other woman, drawing herself up to her petite five-foot height. At that moment I wanted to warn the matchmaker. When my mother was angry it was best not to provoke her.

But the matchmaker wasn't done, "You have ruined my reputation as a reliable matchmaker. Since you walked out, I had to make the apologies..."

I was glad my mother's anger wasn't directed at me as I watched her advance toward the matchmaker. I could only imagine what my mother's expression was because as she drew nearer, the matchmaker took a step back. She looked nervous and held up her hands, as if to protect herself.

"You are done with me?" my mother asked in a cold voice. "How dare you! You bring an old man for my eighteen-year-old girl to marry and expect me to be happy. Leave right now before I throw you out by the hair."

The matchmaker looked completely cowed. She tried to say something but my mother deliberately moved closer to her. The woman took one more look at my mother's face and immediately pulled her sari around her and turned away without another word.

By now Muthi, Devi and Thangam had entered into the kitchen. My mother looked exhausted. I pulled out a wooden stool and she sat down with a heavy sigh.

"What is going on?" both Devi and Muthi asked at the same time, looking at me and then my mother.

I said nothing. I just sat next to my mother and put my hand on hers. She turned my hand around and we held hands just like we used to when I was a child.

"Meena, here is going to college," my mother said looking at me. "But first we are going on a trip."

My eyes filled with tears even as my mouth turned up in a huge smile.

"Oh Amma," I said with a sob and laugh.

We turned to Muthi and Devi who were watching us with wide eyes and open mouths. I laughed out loud at their bewildered expressions. I gestured to Thangam to come sit next to me.

She sat down between my mother and me. My mother smiled at both of us.

"Tonight we will have a special meal, complete with carrot halwa," she said to all of us.

My mother's carrot halva was a tasty mixture of fresh garden carrots, golden ghee, brown sugar and cardamom. I knew the sweet taste of carrot halva would taste more delectable than ever because my mother and I were once again on the same side. We were a team and that feeling was sweeter than any dessert.

CHAPTER 5
FORTUNES TOLD

I woke up the next morning with a feeling of lightness and anticipation. For a second I couldn't recall why I was so happy. It was that feeling I used to get when I knew my father was coming to visit or at the start of school holidays. Even though I missed my father with all my heart, right now my whole body was tingling with joy. Then I remembered what had happened yesterday and felt happiness bloom in my heart like a lotus opening to the morning sun. I jumped out of bed and hurried to the kitchen. It was bustling as usual but I found joy everywhere and the kitchen seemed to be bathed in golden light. I looked around at everything and felt my senses become overwhelmed. The jam jars on the window sill looked like they were filled with jewel-hued fruit instead of plain old plums. The morning sounds coming from the kitchen was like sweet music to my ears. The nutty scent of mustard seeds popping in hot oil and the mouth-watering scent of frying onions made me want to sing and dance. I was delirious with joy.

I hugged Thangam and Appu who were having breakfast before heading off to school. Appu struggled out of my arms but Thangam smiled at me.

"Chechi, we have visitors," she announced.

I looked up at Devi who nodded as she passed me a cup of coffee.

"Go see for yourself," she said, pointing to the front yard.

I walked to the courtyard to peer through the open doorway. Just past the cowsheds, I saw the lower half of our property was filled with horses and colorful caravans.

"The gypsies," I breathed. "Priya's family is here."

Over four years ago I had befriended a gypsy girl named Priya. Priya's father had been unjustly accused of theft and my mother had helped catch the real culprit to prove Priya's father's innocence. Afterwards my mother had invited them to camp on our property. It had been a long time since we had seen Priya and her band of wandering gypsies and I was eager to renew our friendship.

Thangam and I walked down the hill and through the meadow to the lower field. Some of the gypsy men were unloading carts and wiping down their horses. The women were busy building fires and getting the morning meal started in huge iron pots. I saw a young woman with a baby boy on her hip, bending down to stir a pot. When she straightened, our eyes met and I recognized my friend Priya.

"Priya?" I called out. "Is that you? Who is this little one?"

"Hello Meena! You remember my brother Shiva? This is his boy. His name is Surya, my ray of sunshine."

She turned to Thangam and smiled, "How are you Thangam. You look so grown up."

Thangam tried to hide behind me and I put an arm around her shoulders.

The plump boy took his thumb out of his mouth to smile at me. I stroked his bare foot which was soft and smooth to touch.

"He is so handsome," I said. "How are you?"

"I'm doing well. I'm a fortune teller now ever since my granny died."

"You haven't been here in a long time. I have missed you."

"I missed coming to Mahagiri and seeing you but we aren't traveling as much these days," Priya said. "There aren't too many places for us to camp. We are not as welcome. My family has decided to settle down in central India now by a river. We are no longer nomads."

I was sad to hear that the traveling gypsy life style might be coming to an end.

"My mother says you are always welcome here," I reminded her.

"Yes, this is one of the few places we feel welcome, but traveling all this way has become difficult. In fact, this might be the last time to come this way."

"I'm so sad to hear that," I said. "But I'm glad to see you."

She shifted the baby from one hip to the other. "You should come back tonight, Meena, so I can read your palm. That is how I earn some money for us...."

I'm really good," she added with a smile.

"Okay, I'll come back after dinner."

"Can I come too?" Thangam said from my side. I had forgotten she was with me. I looked down into her pleading eyes.

"You should be getting ready for school," I said. "Come on, let's get back before the bus leaves without you."

I said good-bye to Priya and hustled Thangam up the hill. I walked the twins to the bus stand and waved as the bus pulled away.

That night after dinner, I slipped out of the house without Thangam or anyone else noticing. Twilight had come and gone and the first stars of the night were peering out from a velvety black sky. A crescent moon provided enough light as I made my way down the dirt path toward the flickering cooking fires and kerosene lanterns. As I wandered into the encampment, I wondered how I would ever find Priya in this semi-darkness.

"Meena," a voice called out. "Over here."

I looked in the direction of the voice and saw Priya, seated on the steps of the parked horse cart. She got up when I approached and beckoned me inside. I had never been inside a gypsy cart and was surprised to find it was quite spacious. A kerosene lantern hung from a beam and cast a warm glow and I could see most of the space was taken up by a huge mattress. One side of the cart was covered with a thick rug piled high with many pillows and blankets. Priya pulled out a cushion and indicated to me to sit down. She sat on a blanket and shoved a pillow behind her back.

"There that is better," she said with a sigh. "I have been on my feet all day, taking care of the little ones. They're always a little fussy in a new place."

Priya held out her hands. "Now, let's see what the future holds for you, Meena. Come closer and give me your palms."

I scooted closer. She grasped my hands in her warm little hands and studied each palm for a long moment and then she sighed and released me.

"Well, Meena," she said with a smile. "Your future is looking a little hazy."

I laughed. "You probably say that about everyone."

"You are skeptical?" she asked me. "Alright, what if I tell you that you will be traveling soon to a place that smells like sweet cardamom?"

"What are you talking about?" I asked. "I haven't made any plans..."

Priya smiled, a little smugly. "I know you will travel with a man with blue eyes. There is another longer voyage in your future."

"I can't believe you read all of that from my just looking at my palm," I said. "I'm a believer now."

Priya laughed. "Meena, your future looks good to me. I even see you making a meal for me."

I had to laugh too. The lone hoot of an owl reminded me it was getting late.

"I better get back to the house before my mother sends out a search party," I said. "Bring your family to dinner before you leave."

"That will be a treat. I still remember the coconut rice you served us last time."

I walked up the hill and found Thangam sitting on the front porch. She had a frown on her face.

"You left me behind, Chechi," she said. "Then Amma wouldn't let me go by myself."

"I'm sorry, little one," I said. "But Priya will be coming to dinner and you can visit with her and play with her nephew."

She smiled at me, "Alright, chechi."

CHAPTER 6
A FEAST FOR MAC

Now that my mother and I had put aside our differences I began to spend a lot of time in the kitchen. The end of the summer harvest was starting to come in. Bhojan and Kashi brought in baskets of beans, the pale pink striped pods bursting open to reveal the creamy colored beans inside. These beans would be dried and used in curries and sauces in the winter months. My mother and Devi liked to make jam with the peaches and plums. The jars of yellow and ruby red preserves were colorful addition to our kitchen. For the past few years, my mother had been selling these jams and jellies to her milk customers. She had become a busy and successful businesswoman.

Working in the kitchen, alongside Devi, Muthi and my mother, I realized how much I enjoyed being in this old room. I loved the kitchen for its warmth and rich aromas of cooking and spices. When it was filled with laughter and activity, as it was right now, the kitchen was a magical place of transformation and joy. I had invited Mac for dinner and my mother had insisted we prepare a proper feast.

"After all, I have to thank him for taking care of you when I had lost my way," she said.

Muthi added, "I hope he brings Mala. She likes our spicy food."

As soon as the twins left for school, I had joined the women in the kitchen. I helped cut a huge pumpkin into small chunks. The seeds were saved to be roasted and rubbed with salt and pepper, a perfect after-school snack for the twins. The pumpkin was stewed in coconut milk and cumin. Today, my mother added a handful of cooked white beans and laced the fragrant sauce with warm coconut oil and sprigs of fresh curry leaves. Along with the pumpkin curry, my mother had Muthi chop a mountain of fresh green beans into tiny bits. The cut beans, green as jade, were crisp and fresh. They would be sautéed with onions, peppers, and mustard seeds. Fresh coconut scrapings, sea salt and turmeric would be added for flavor and color. My mother decided to make her famous pepper broth, pungent with fresh garlic and black pepper. Devi fried lentil wafers into delicate papadams, a perfect accompaniment for the spicy pepper broth. There was also mild and delicious coconut potato stew, steaming hot Basmati rice and golden ghee. For dessert my mother decided on the creamy vermicelli pudding. This pudding flavored with toasted cashews, fresh cardamom powder and plump raisins was a family favorite.

"We will have to save some of this delicious food for the twins," I said. "They will be unhappy to have missed the feast."

"There is plenty," Devi said as she placed a platter of fried papadams on the table.

When Mac and Mala arrived for the feast my mother had decided to serve the food on traditional banana leaves but took pity of Mac and gave him a spoon and fork. Muthi and my mother preferred scooping up the rice and sauces with their fingers but Mac and I used the spoons and forks to eat our food. We were enjoying the sweet pudding when Mac finally asked the question that was on everyone's mind.

"So, Sudha," he addressed my mother, "what changed your mind?"

My mother licked the last drop of pudding from her fingers and was quiet for a long moment, gathering her thoughts. Finally, she looked up at Mac.

"When I was standing in that living room and watching my beautiful Meena sitting next to a stranger who was trying to convince her that her son was the perfect groom for her, it was like I had an out of body experience. I can't explain the feeling. Meena, I think your father was standing right there beside me and that is when I realized how selfish I was being.

"Instead of grooming you to be an independent and self-reliant woman, I was trying to mold you into a woman who would be dependent on a stranger for her well-being. What kind of mother does that?"

My mother shook her head and we all sat frozen in our seats as we listened to her heart-felt words.

She looked at me now as she spoke, "Your father was whispering in my ear that I had to do everything in my power to make sure you grew up into a self-confident woman. To ensure that education was the key, not marriage to a complete stranger."

My mother turned to Mac, "That is when I realized I was being stubborn and old-fashioned and you were right. We need to make sure my husband's farm is his legacy. It will be a testament to his love for the land and the people."

Mac smiled and his blue eyes looked brighter than ever. "Sudha, I never doubted your love for Meena. Even when she came to me to ask for advice she never criticized you or what you were doing. She just wants to experience a different life."

I cleared my throat. "Really, Mac," I said. "No need to talk as if I'm not here. I'll admit I was very angry with my mother but I always knew she wanted what was best for me. Now, I'm so happy that we both want the same things. So, when can we go to the plantation?"

Both my mother and Mac laughed.

"She was always impatient," my mother said. "I would like to come with you and say good-bye to the place that was so important to my husband. How about we leave in about a week?"

I was surprised my mother wanted to come but I was glad that both of us would go to my father's plantation together.

"We should bring the twins," I said. "They need to see their father's place and we can stop at the Nature Preserve."

Mac rubbed his hands together. "It will be a holiday."

"The twins will have to miss school and I will need to meet with the head mistress," my mother said. "We might need more than a week to plan this trip."

"A fortnight, then?" Mac asked.

My mother nodded and as soon as Mac left, she and Muthi started to discuss everything that needed to be done before the upcoming trip, but I tuned them out. My heart was singing because I was going to be with my mother and together we would make sure my father's legacy will be kept intact for many, many years to come.

CHAPTER 7
SCHOOL FRIEND

I had been friends with Kumari Sen since we first met in kindergarten. Over the years, we had spent countless hours at each other's homes. In fact Kumari and I had been having a sleepover when we caught Jaibal sneaking into our kitchen. We still liked to tease Jaibal about that night. Now Kumari was getting ready to go study drama in New York and we had been planning this visit for a long time. We had hoped we would somehow get together in America.

"Tell me again why you are going to your father's estate?" she asked.

I then told her about my seeing ceremony and the shock of the old man.

Kumari giggled. "Oh my, I can't imagine what you thought, you must have been so glad when your mother took you away from that room."

"I was," I agreed. "But it was a huge shock to see the groom, though I think he was actually a nice man who was just too old for me.'"

Kumari loved hearing about my plans.

"Your father would be so proud of you, Meena," she said in a wistful tone.

Her own father was a hard-to-please diplomat and I didn't envy my friend.

"What about you?" I asked her. "Is your family arranging your marriage?"

She shrugged her shoulders, "They will as soon as I'm done with college."

"Don't you care?"

I was surprised by her answer, "Not really. I know my mother will choose a suitable boy and really, Meena, I don't see marriage as being that big a deal. Your parents' marriage was so different from mine. My parents lead separate lives and I think my father may even have another family somewhere else. Don't look so shocked."

"But...."

"He is away a lot and has to travel abroad all the time and so I think my mother doesn't mind."

I shook my head. My mother and father had been devoted to each other. The story of their courtship had been one of my favorite childhood stories.

My parents had come to Mahagiri for their honeymoon and my mother had fallen in love with the clear air and blue skies of this hilltop town. My father loved my mother so much he agreed to let her live in Mahagiri while he built a suitable house for her on his plantation. He had even bought her this bungalow where my mother had started a thriving milk business. Over the years she had become a fixture in the town and my father didn't want to take her away from her life in Mahagiri and so he became a "second Saturday husband" visiting his family once a month. I had always looked forward to his monthly visits. Until his death my mother and father had never been apart for more than a few weeks at a time.

Muthi interrupted my thoughts. "Meena and Kumari, would you like to help in the kitchen?"

I didn't want to, but Kumari loved working in our kitchen.

"Oh yes, Muthi, what is going on today?"

"We are making tomato jam with the last of the summer tomatoes and need a person to stir the pot," Muthi said.

I had forgotten we were supposed to make jam. We had already peeled and seeded the tomatoes in preparation for making jam.

Soon Kumari and I were busy stirring the boiling mixture. The kitchen was warm and steamy with scent of sweet tomato jam. We left the jars cooling in their water bath and walked to the back of the house.

Our backyard was an oasis of calm that only comes from things growing in the soil. Right now the last of the potatoes and carrots were being harvested. Cabbage, cauliflower and garlic waited to be planted before the winter chill.

Devi brought us a plate of brown bread with still-warm tomato jam and Kumari and I happily munched on the tasty snack. Muthi's cardamom tea was the perfect accompaniment to the bread and jam.

"I'll always remember this time with you, Meena," Kumari said as she swallowed the last of the bread. "We are both going on great adventures soon. You will have to come visit me in New York."

I put down my plate and mug and hugged my friend.

"I'll miss you and I really want to visit you."

CHAPTER 8
MEMORY LANE

THE STORY OF LORD RAMA AND THE BOATMAN

On his way to his exile to the forest, Lord Rama, his wife Seetha and his brother had to cross a river. They were met by Guha, king of the boat people, who offered to row the Lord across the river. Guha asked one of his trusted boatmen to take Lord Rama in his boat but the boatman insisted that he would like to wash Lord Rama's feet before he climbed into the little wooden vessel. Everyone was getting a little tired of the boatman's stubborn request, so Lord Rama asked the boatman the reason for his demand.

"Lord," said the boatman. "I would like to wash your feet before you enter my boat because I have heard that the dust from your feet when it touched a pebble becomes a woman. My boat is made of wood and I'm afraid that the dust from your feet will create so many women that I will not be able to provide for all of them."

Lord Rama was touched by the boatman's innocent but firm faith. He allowed the boatman to wash his feet and anoint his head. Lord Rama blessed the boatman so he would never have to worry about taking care of his family."

—As told by Muthi.

The next few days were filled with fun and excitement as we planned and packed for our upcoming trip. The twins had never been on an extended trip and were so full of joy they were like puppies, constantly getting underfoot. We had decided that Jaibal would drive us to Chandur with a one-night stop at the Nature Preserve. I couldn't wait to re-live my visit to the Preserve. The last time I had been there had been with my father and the trek into the jungle had been memorable. My mother was determined to make this trip a happy one and so I was content to let her take care of all the arrangements. For the first time in months it felt like my life was moving forward. My future looked much brighter than it did a week ago.

Finally the day of the trip arrived. Bhojan and Mac sat in the front with Jaibal while my mother and I were with the twins in the back. Muthi and Devi waved good-bye and soon we were off.

"Achan, always stopped in Greater Mahagiri," I said to the twins as Jaibal pulled the car into the busy bus station parking lot. He found a spot right next to a stone building. I stepped out of the car and looked down at the creek just below the restroom. My mother, Thangam and I walked into the ladies room and the pungent scent of urine and feces was as disgusting as I remembered. I wondered if Appu's experience next door was any better.

Jaibal was waiting by the car with a long garland of jasmine buds in his hands.

"You remembered," I said as I plunged my nose into the sweet smelling blooms.

"The master always bought flowers after we used the restroom," Jaibal explained to my mother. "It was a way to get rid of the smell and to fill our noses and the car with jasmine flowers."

He laid another garland on the front dash of the car which was soon filled with the sweet scent. I looked up to see Mac and Bhojan coming toward us. Bhojan had a paper bag in his hand.

"Varkees?" He held out the bag which was filled with flaky varkee, a roll that was a perfect blend of sweet and savory flavors.

I was touched by how each of them was trying to make this journey as memorable as possible. This was going to be a nostalgic and emotional trip for me. It was a fitting way to honor and remember my father.

"How about having some chai to go with that?" Mac asked. He passed us small glass tumblers filled with creamy sweet tea.

"Not your *cuppa?*" I asked.

He laughed.

"You know, when in Rome...." He sipped his hot tea.

Soon we were back on the road. I advised the twins to lie down as we started making our way down the hill. The steep U-bends could cause nausea. It was quiet in the car as the twins dozed off and I was able to look out at the passing scenery without interruptions. The road was a single-lane highway now with a deep gully on one side. I glanced up to my right where the rocky slope was filled with sparse vegetation. Trees and shrubs seemed to hang on the hillside, clinging in desperation. I had heard this road was often blocked by mudslides during the monsoon rains. It was easy to imagine the trees and shrubs sliding down the hillsides. It was starting to get warmer now and I struggled out of my sweater. Jaibal rolled down the windows and warm air wafted in but it was not as refreshing as the cool breezes of Mahagiri.

I nudged my sister awake. "We are almost there," She sat up and I turned to Appu who was already looking out the window.

"Welcome to South India's Largest Nature Preserve." He read the sign out loud.

Thangam read the one about littering.

"Why aren't plastic bags allowed in the Preserve, Chechi?" she asked me.

"Because plastic takes a long time to break down in the soil and when animals eat it they become sick."

"They don't know not to eat them?"

"I think sometimes they think it is food because it smells like leftover food and other times they just eat it by accident and it gets stuck in their stomachs because they can't digest plastic."

"I'll make sure all the plastic bags are put away," she promised.

It seemed like things hadn't changed around here. We stopped at a small gatehouse, manned by a uniformed guard. He waved us through after Jaibal showed him our reservation.

"Follow the path to the Mountainside Nature Preserve," he instructed Jaibal.

The front office was a large wooden building and as we pulled up the curved driveway, another uniformed guard hurried out to open our doors. We all wanted to jump out and stretch our legs.

My mother turned to me, "Meena, Mac and I'll go check us in. You keep an eye on the twins."

"Come out, you two," I said.

The air was warm and thick and very different from Mahagiri.

"It's so hot here," Thangam said, pulling her thick braid off her neck.

"We can walk down that path," I said, pointing to a trail. "Let's stay close until Amma comes back."

We wandered down the path. Appu froze when he heard the scream of a wild creature in the woods beyond the path.

"What was that?" he asked, a little alarmed.

"I'm not sure," I replied. "There are all kinds of creatures in the jungle. That's why we have to stay close to the houses."

My mother came back with a set of keys with Mac right behind her.

"Mac and I checked us in," my mother said, handing him a set of keys.

"Amma, we'll take this path to the guesthouse. We can stretch our legs and meet you at the guesthouse in a few minutes."

"I'll go with them, Sudha," Mac said.

The four of us walked down a dirt path. Mac stepped ahead to open a wooden gate.

"I can close it, Mac," Appu said.

We followed the path around a manicured lawn to a row of about a dozen cabins. There seemed to be more guesthouses than I remembered from my previous visit. Each cabin was sparkling white and had a tiled roof. The cabins had front porches with a wooden bench, a chair and a small table. My mother was already waiting for us at a cabin with a blue door.

"Mac, you are right next door," she said pointing to a nearby cabin with a yellow door. "Jaibal and Bhojan are in the one with the green door."

My mother had the door open and I could see this cabin was a little bigger than the one I had shared with my father and Muthi. There were two bedrooms, a bathroom and a small living room. The double beds occupied most of the space in each bedroom and had plaid blankets draped over them. The bathroom had a sink and a Western style toilet which was new. There was also a shower attached to a small water heater. So now we had hot water for showers, again a new addition to the cabin. The last time a maid had to bring hot water in a plastic bucket for me to bathe.

"I'm hungry," Appu said.

"All right, let's go get some food," my mother said.

"Meena, go next door and see if Mac, and men want to join us."

I walked out onto the porch and looked down the path. The orange marigolds and red wildflowers made the place welcoming and colorful but I was still mindful that the jungle was just a few feet away. Mac was on the porch, puffing on his pipe. He waved and I waved back, "Do you want to join us for lunch?"

He put out his pipe and placed it on the bench and came down the porch steps.

"Bhojan has already gone with Jaibal to wash the car," he said. "I thought I'd wait for you."

"I'm glad you did," I smiled at him. "Coming back here is a little hard."

"Thinking of your dad, eh lass?"

I nodded. "We stayed here and walked down this same path to the restaurant."

"It's always good to have memories, lass. Hold fast to them."

Before I could say anything, we were joined by the twins and my mother. The dining room was not crowded and we found a large table by the window.

"Please don't open the windows," the waiter cautioned us as he handed us menus.

"Why?" Thangam asked her eyes wide.

The waiter pointed outside. "See those monkeys on that tree?"

"I see them," Thangam said in an excited voice.

"They are not pets," the waiter said sternly. "They will come in and grab food right from your hands."

"The last time I was here," I said opening the menu, "we had a thali plate."

Mac put down his menu. "Let's have that then." Meena, you can order for me."

So we ordered thali plate lunches for all of us. The food was as delicious as I remembered. There was a huge mound of piping hot white rice, golden ghee, smoky eggplant gravy, carrot and beans with shredded coconut, crispy rice wafers, spicy mango pickle and sweet pudding for dessert. We were all hungry and dug in. For a few moments the only sounds were those of eating and chewing. It was quiet and peaceful at our table.

After lunch we walked to the side of the dining room to a long stone terrace. There were chairs and tables, some in the dappled shade of large trees. I sat down with my mother and Mac, while the twins perched on the short wall.

"I've reserved a jeep ride tonight and an elephant ride tomorrow morning," my mother told us.

Mac nodded. "That sounds great."

"I'll walk with the twins if you two want to get a bit of rest," I offered.

"All right," Mac said as he pushed himself off the chair.

The twins and I spent the next hour exploring the Preserve. We walked and sometimes ran down the paths. When we were finally hot and tired, we wandered inside and found a small museum. We browsed through all the exhibits and read about the animals found at the Nature Preserve.

"We'd better head back to the cabin," I said. "Amma may worry."

Mac was nowhere to be seen but my mother was on the porch, reading a magazine. She looked up as we came up the path.

"Come sit down and have a cold drink," she said, pointing to a pitcher of lemonade.

I left the twins with her and walked inside. After using the bathroom, I lay down on the bed and closed my eyes.

"Meena, wake up." Thangam was shaking my shoulder. "Time for tea and then we are going into the jungle.

I stretched and yawned. The nap had felt good but I slept longer than I should. I splashed water on my face and followed the sound of voices to the porch. The sun was lower in the horizon and daylight was fading.

My mother was pouring tea. The familiar silver tray containing a steaming pot of black tea, a jug of warm milk, a container of white sugar and several cups and saucers was on the wooden table. Mac had joined us.

"I guess we old'uns had to take a nap," he said with a twinkle in his eye.

I laughed and sat down next to him.

"I don't know about you but a nap was just the thing. "Where are the men?"

"They are too shy to come join us," Mac said. "So I sent them to have tea in the dining room. They are happy to sit there."

"I guess they don't want to see elephants and tigers?" I asked.

Mac laughed. "Not at all. I think they plan to stay inside."

My mother handed me a cup of tea. I added some sugar and picked up a strawberry jam sandwich.

"The green ones are spicy," Thangam complained. "My mouth is burning."

The cilantro pesto and cucumber sandwiches were indeed spicy but I loved the hot tangy taste.

"Ginger scones are better," Mac grumbled.

We finished our tea and I told my mother about the oil Muthi had insisted I pack. This mixture of eucalyptus and citrus oils was supposed to keep bugs and mosquitoes away from us. I showed the twins how to rub some on their palms and use it on their necks, faces and other exposed parts of their bodies.

Appu crinkled his nose. "We stink."

"Yes, we do," my mother said, "But we won't get bitten either."

With that we joined Mac and walked down to where an open-air jeep was waiting.

As we bumped through the darkening jungle, I was so acutely reminded of the last time I was here with my father. I tried not to give in to those memories and instead enjoyed watching the twins getting excited about seeing herds of deer, wild buffalo and water birds. When we returned to the guest house, night had fallen on the Preserve and we were glad to sip bowls of hot tomato soup on our porch before going to bed.

It seemed as if we had all just gotten into bed when there was a knock on our door.

"Time for the dawn ride," a polite employee from the Preserve told us. "We'll serve you coffee on the ride."

Surprisingly the twins didn't grumble at being awakened so early. It was cool outside and the last of the stars could be seen twinkling in the night sky. We rode in the Jeep for a short distance. In the semi-darkness the elephants were large silhouettes etched out in quiet splendor against the morning sky. We watched the elephants being readied as we sipped on hot coffee.

We were eventually assisted up to a wooden platform and then onto the sturdy back of an elephant. The elephant's mahout was standing next to the large animal, keeping him calm with clicks and soothing sounds. My mother struggled a bit to get onto the elephant but soon we were all settled on a make-shift bench made of bamboo, rugs and old pieces of cloth. It smelled of animals and dried sweat. There was a bamboo railing on either side of the platform and I joined the twins, holding onto the bamboo railing, my feet dangling over the elephant's side.

Time has a way of slowing down when you are on an elephant ride. There was no rushing the huge beast. You just have to sit back and enjoy the slow swaying movement. It was a hypnotic ride into the still-dark jungle. I looked up at the eastern sky which was turning into a golden yellow. The orange sun was just peeking over the horizon. Morning was arriving at the Nature Preserve. Soon we were deep in the silent jungle surrounded by teak trees. The mahout pointed and we strained our eyes to see a herd of water buffalo, stomping and snorting at the edge of a watering hole. We went further into the jungle and the silence was deafening when our guide abruptly stopped the elephant. That is when we caught a glimpse of bright orange among the dark green. A tiger? We sat, our mouths a little agape, as the cat leaped high into a tree. It vanished as suddenly as it had appeared. We all let out a breath we didn't know we had been holding. It seemed like the entire jungle also let out a sigh of relief. Even the elephant seemed to be relieved and let out a loud fart which had the twins in giggles. I longed for one more glimpse of the grace and power of the jungle cat but we never saw the tiger again. Somehow the rest of the trek seemed anti-climactic to me. The sun was bright and the air was warm when we arrived back to our rooms. We stopped at the dining hall for a quick breakfast and soon we were on our way to Chandur.

CHAPTER 9
CHANDUR

As we drove down the highway, we passed a small shack and truck stop. I caught Jaibal's eye in the rearview mirror.

"Is that the place?"

He nodded.

I twisted back in my seat to catch a glimpse of the wooden shack or roadside restaurant as my father called it. On my last visit my father had stopped here for what he called the best breakfast. The herb omelet on a toasted buttery bun with hot coffee had been a delicious breakfast. I glanced at my mother and knew that she would never approve of eating at a roadside stall. I sighed and sat back. I guess some memories will have to remain just memories. But I could taste the crunchy roll, the creamy egg and the sharp tang of fresh herbs.

A few hours later, we arrived at the outskirts of Chandur. There was a small inn here, owned by a widow named Saraswathi. The men planned to stay here. Jaibal was going to drive us to the plantation before checking in. Saraswathi welcomed us and showed the men to their rooms.

"Would you please stay for lunch?" she asked.

Breakfast seemed a long time ago and we agreed.

I was glad we did because the lunch was simple with a delicate delicious touch. There was fresh whole wheat bread, steaming white rice, a rich dal soup flavored with green onions and cumin seeds and cabbage in a yogurt sauce. We finished with cups of cardamom tea and shortbread-like cookies made from chickpea flour.

"The spices are from your husband's place," Saraswathi told my mother. "He was an honest and good man."

My mother smiled, and I left the women to chat. I found Mac on the front porch with the twins.

"Ah, there you are," he said.

I sat on the wooden bench next to Appu.

"So what is the plan?" I asked. "When will your friend be here?"

"He said he will arrive tonight. He plans to stay here as well. We will meet tomorrow afternoon with you and your mother."

I didn't say anything for a moment.

"Not having second thoughts about selling the place, are ye lass?"

I shook my head, "No, but being here is bringing back a lot of memories."

"Like what, Chechi," Appu asked.

I looked down at him, "Well, it just reminds me of Achan and how much I miss him. I'm looking forward to showing you the spice plantation. We can go on a hike up to the top of the hill."

We took leave of Mac and Bhojan and my mother promised to visit Saraswathi again.

The long driveway and the bumpy road to the farmstead was a familiar homecoming that brought a lump to my throat. My father should have been here welcoming us. My father's house was a two-story structure with an open veranda on the ground floor. This porch was surrounded by a white-washed low wall that was wide enough to sit on. We had just opened the car doors when I heard my name. I got out and saw a figure running down the slope.

"Meena, is that really you?" a familiar voice called out.

My friend Radha and her father Murthy were hurrying to welcome us.

"Radha," I said. "Come meet my family."

I introduced everyone and Murthy greeted my mother and Bhojan.

"Little Mother, we have heard so much about you," he said, putting his palms together in a gesture of respect.

"Meena, we should go on a hike," Radha said. "And I want to go up the hill…"

She was interrupted by her mother Paru Amma.

"Radha, let the girl breathe," she said coming toward me with a smile.

I remembered her kind face and the large nose ring in her left nostril. She wore a dark blue saree, the end draped over her head and shoulder.

"Paru Amma," I said, taking her work worn hands in mine.

"We were so sorry about your father, Meena. I wanted to come but Murthy said your father would have preferred we stay and keep the farm going."

"You have been doing a great job," I assured. "Come meet my mother."

"Little Mother," Paru Amma said with reverence. "Your husband spoke of you all the time. Come sit down and let me get you some cardamom tea or coffee."

We were soon settled on the veranda with steaming cups of cardamom coffee. As I took a long sip of the fragrant drink with an unusual flavor, I silently toasted my father. This was truly a pilgrimage in his memory.

That night we all ate in the smoky kitchen on a low wooden table. Even Jaibal joined us before heading back to Saraswathi's. I met Anand, a young bookkeeper, and his betrothed a fiery young woman named Rani. I noticed Jaibal and Radha exchanging glances. Was a romance brewing?

The food was delicious. There were several curries, fresh bread, mango and lemon pickle and later cups of vanilla flavored milk.

That night we all slept well. I felt secure and comfortable, enveloped in my father's love.

CHAPTER 10
PLANTATION LIFE

The next morning I wandered outside to find my mother sitting on the veranda having tea with Murthy. I joined them, helping myself to a cup of warm spiced scented tea, from the steel tea pot. I inhaled the rich cardamom and pepper flavors, the essence of the plantation.

"I was just explaining to Murthy what our plans were for the place," my mother said to me.

"If you are satisfied, Little Mother, we are happy too," Murthy said. "My time as manager of this place has been rewarding. Your husband took me in when I thought I had no prospects. He changed my family's lives."

"Murthy here was just telling me his story and how a man named Veerasamy was giving your father a hard time."

I looked at Murthy with a questioning look, "Who is Veerasamy?"

"Veerasamy was the manager of this estate before me. He was fired by your father, Meena, when he learned that Veerasamy was threatening the laborers. He asked for bribes from workers if they wanted to keep their jobs. Things were pretty bad when your father first came here. He had to gain the trust of the laborers and I was one of his most vocal critics. He won me over with the way he managed the place. He never complained. He worked in the fields, picking or sorting spices. He worked in the kiln room and he drove a lorry with supplies when it was needed. I found his honesty and hard work so refreshing that I offered to help him. He hired me to be the manager and Paru Amma and I have been here a long time."

"You are really part of this place," I said. "You should meet with the buyer and we won't make any decision without consulting you. Right, Amma?"

"I think that is wise," my mother said.

Murthy bowed his head. "I'm honored to be included."

When the twins woke up we had breakfast on the veranda. We enjoyed rice dumplings with spicy coconut chutney and a variety of fresh fruits, all accompanied by more tea.

After breakfast Radha offered to take the twins around the estate and my mother and I sat on the veranda, waiting for Mac and his friend to arrive. We didn't have to wait long. Jaibal pulled into the driveway and opened the doors to let his passengers out. Mac and a distinguished looking older man climbed out of the car.

My mother and I walked down the porch to greet our visitors. I went ahead to hug Mac.

"Mac, welcome to my father's plantation," I said.

"Meena, I want you to meet my dear friend Nandan," he said, still holding on to my hands.

I smiled at the gentleman who looked at me with a twinkle in his eye.

"I could have guessed you were Meena from all of Mac's descriptions. Good to meet you young lady."

I smiled, feeling a little shy. Then I felt my mother's reassuring arm around me.

"Little Mother," Nandan said with a courtly bow.

My mother laughed, "Please call me Sudha. That name was given to me many years ago and somehow it has stuck."

"Sudha," Nandan acknowledged. "Thank you for inviting me to this lovely place."

We walked together as a group to the veranda where Murthy stood, waiting like a guardian of the estate.

He greeted Nandan with his palms together.

"Namashkaram, sir. Welcome to our home."

Once we were all seated, Murthy waved to Rani who was coming out of the house with cleaning supplies.

"Rani, please tell Paru Amma we would like some tea."

The girl nodded and walked down the path to the kitchen.

"Looks like you have quite the operation here," Nandan said.

Murthy nodded, "We grow cardamom, cashews, black pepper and some vanilla pods. The cardamom is processed here. I can show you the drying shed but we send out the cashews, black and vanilla to several merchants who clean and sell the products. We have also planted coffee bushes on some hillsides. I knew the master wanted to expand that part of the estate but he died before we finished our plans. I have the estate maps here that show where the crops are planted and our picking schedule."

He laid out several pieces of paper and a thick binder. Nandan got up to look at the maps. Paru Amma and Rani came up to the veranda with a tray of spice tea and snacks. Once everyone was served, Nandan turned to my mother.

"Are you willing to sell the place, Sudha? After all, isn't this your husband's legacy?"

"It was not an easy decision but my life is in Mahagiri with the children and my business. It has always been. Can you believe it this is my first visit to the estate? I wanted to come when my husband was alive but I was always too busy. I think selling to a friend of Mac's will be a good thing."

Nandan nodded and looked at Bhojan and Murthy, "As you know I want to eventually turn this into a spice co-op and it will be part of a larger co-op I'm working on with several farms and merchants. This means that laborers will be able to purchase a share of the co-op and be responsible for the day-to-day management of the place. Do you think your workers will be interested in this?"

Murthy rubbed his chin as he thought about Nandan's question.

"I think they will be more than willing to listen. Perhaps we can hold a meeting tomorrow? They were all happy to work for the master because he was fair and his wages were the highest in the area."

"A meeting is a good idea," Nandan said. "I can stay for another day or two. What do you think, Mac?"

Mac nodded, "I can stay. I know Sudha and her wee ones are going to be here until the end of the week."

After tea, Murthy took Nandan on a tour of the kiln and the part of the estate close to the house. I sat on the veranda with my mother and Mac.

"He seems like a reasonable man," my mother said referring to Nandan.

"Sudha, I have known him for a long time and he is a good family man. He is that rare combination: an honest businessman."

Our conversation was interrupted by the arrival of Radha and the twins.

"Amma, chechi, we saw some tribal people and they invited us to their village," Appu said.

"Hello Appu, Thangam," Mac greeted them.

They paused to greet him Mac and hug him. But they quickly turned to my mother.

"So can we go?"

We smiled at their enthusiasm.

"We can talk about it later. Right now we have visitors and you two need to wash up," she said.

Appu looked as if he was going to argue until I bent down and whispered in his ear, "Appu, leave it to me. I want to visit the village too and I'll convince Amma."

He brightened and went off to wash up.

Paru Amma, Radha and Rani served lunch on the veranda. Paru Amma's idea of a simple menu was a number of delicious dishes. I wasn't complaining as I dug into coconut rice, fiery pepper rice, tangy lemon rice and soothing yogurt rice along with several vegetable dishes including Paru Amma's famous cabbage stir-fry. For dessert there was creamy cardamom pudding and vanilla kefir.

"Radha, tell me about the tribal people," I asked my friend as she was serving us hot tea.

"They live a day's walk in the jungle and are very friendly. They respected your father," she said. "I heard scary stories about them when I was a child but one day I met one of them and she was so nice. Her name was Chella and today when we were hiking we met her husband and he invited the twins to the village for a meal."

"I would love to see the village," I said a little wistfully.

My mother looked over at me, "Meena, you can go with the twins and Radha and perhaps one of the other estate workers, can also accompany you."

I was surprised by my mother's suggestion. She was not usually so happy to let us out her sight.

She must have seen the astonished look on my face because she said, "I think it will be a good adventure for the twins and you. Radha, can you do this trip in one day?"

"Little Mother, it is too far to come back in one day. The tribal people are used to walking long distances but I think we should stay the night and Chella's husband even suggested that."

"How will you know where to go?" my mother asked her.

"Chella's husband, Kariappan, will be in the area until tomorrow. I told him he was welcome to come here for a meal so you can meet him and talk to him."

My mother nodded, "Alright, I'll talk to him and if I feel comfortable you can go with him tomorrow afternoon."

The twins were so excited. They went to play with some of the laborers' children and we watched them run around in the front yard.

Nandan, Jaibal and Mac left after afternoon tea, promising to come back tomorrow to talk to the farm workers and iron out the legalities of the sale.

That evening my mother and I decided to go for a walk. We hiked the slope, passing the bright green cardamom plants, the pepper vines and the vanilla bean stalks.

We reached the top of the hill and stood side by side looking down at the estate. The evening sun was just setting over the tree tops. The day was coming to an end and the valley below us was bathed in the warm glow of the setting sun. We sighed simultaneously and smiled at each other.

My mother swept her arm toward the estate lying below us. "This is your father's legacy, Meenakutty."

I nodded, not trusting myself to speak because of the lump in my throat.

"I hope he will approve of us selling it," I finally said.

"I think he will," my mother said softly. "I will carry his memory of this place with me to Mahagiri."

She turned, "Keep an eye on your brother and sister on your adventure to the tribal village. They can be a handful."

I laughed out loud, the lump of sorrow dissolving in my throat, "Don't I know it. I was surprised when you agreed."

She shook her head, "This is probably our last visit here and I wanted to give them an experience they will never forget. A trip to the village will certainly be that."

I had to agree. We stood for a moment longer and I took a deep breath as I gazed down into the valley. The lush landscape below me reminded me sharply of my father. *Goodbye Acha.* Both of us were silent as we made our way down the slope.

CHAPTER 11
FATHER'S LEGACY

The next morning after breakfast the twins rushed off to wait for Kariappan. I accompanied my mother on a tour of the plantation. The kiln room was warm and fragrant, a little like being cocooned in a cardamom pod.

"I could live here," I said breathing in the intoxicating scent.

"If you did you would never eat another cardamom pod," Murthy joked. "Sometimes we can't drink a drop of spice tea."

The twins met us at the farmhouse, accompanied by an older gentleman.

"This is Kariappan uncle," Radha said, using a term of reverence. "He is the tribal elder I told you about."

I had expected a fierce looking tribal leader, perhaps with an impressive moustache, and was a little disappointed to see how ordinary he looked. He had the look of an elderly uncle with his weather-beaten face and wrinkled countenance. His eyes, however, were bright and his moustache was neatly trimmed. He wore a colorful cloth tied around his waist and a heavy cotton shirt. A bright yellow turban was wrapped around his head.

"This is Little Mother," Radha said.

He bowed down to my mother, "We all respected your husband," he said in a gravelly voice. He spoke in the local dialect and luckily we were all able to understand him.

"I met him when a cousin and I were passing through the area. It began to rain and there was a violent thunderstorm. Your husband made us feel welcome and gave us shelter and food. After that I always stopped by to pay my respects. Today, I have some honey from our trees."

He pulled out a package wrapped in newspaper that was damp and sticky. The sweet floral smell of the honey filled the air.

My mother accepted the gift.

"My children say they would love to visit your village. Did you really invite them or are they hoping you will?"

"These children are telling the truth, I did invite them to come to our village. I would like you to come too."

"That's very kind of you. Unfortunately I have business to conduct. We are thinking of selling this estate."

The man looked upset at my mother's words.

"Little Mother, is that a good idea? The master would not like a stranger to take over this place."

"No, no Kariappan. This man is a good man and will take care of the plantation and the workers. You can meet him here and have lunch with us before you leave."

Kariappan bowed, "I will be honored to eat with you, Little Mother. And I will bring your children back safely. We will leave this afternoon and should reach our village by nightfall."

"My older daughter, Meena, will also be going."

"Our village is small but our hearts are big and our cooking pots always full," Kariappan said with pride.

A few hours later, Mac's car drove up the long driveway. I watched Nandan get out and take a deep whiff of the warm air. He smiled to himself and walked up to the house with Mac.

"Ah, Meena," he said. "This air satisfies my spirit. I can feel the spice and fragrance flowing through my blood, strengthening me from the inside. I love this place and what it does for my soul."

That is when I realized we had made the right decision in selling my father's planation to Nandan. He was a special man and would make a good caretaker. His next words confirmed my theory.

"I can't wait to share this estate with my wife and daughters. They need to experience the smell of spice and the fragrant winds. My son unfortunately is abroad but I think he will take to this place too. There is so much to experience on this plantation from the spice production to the lovely treks around the estate. The hills must afford great vistas and views and I'm sure my family will enjoy walking on this property. Is everything set for your trip to the village?"

I nodded my head, "Yes. We are planning on leaving after lunch. I'd like you to meet someone."

I motioned to Kariappan who was squatting in the shade of a large pepper tree. He got up and came toward us.

"This is man who is going to buy the plantation," I told him in his dialect. "He says the smell of this place fills his heart."

Kariappan smiled and I had to admire his pearly white teeth which looked like Chiclets to me.

"Then he is the one," he declared.

I translated his statement for Nandan who beamed and leaned forward to shake Kariappan's hand. Bhojan came forward to translate and I left them talking and gesturing.

Lunch was served outside on a large wooden table. We all sat in the dappled shade and enjoyed crisp dosas, a kind of rice crepe, filled with spicy potatoes. The cool yogurt drink, flavored with sharp black pepper and salt, was perfect for the hot afternoon.

"Have you tried taal?" Paru Amma asked bringing out a basket of strange looking brown fruit.

"What is this?" Nandan asked.

My mother replied, "It's a type of palm fruit. You have to peel the brown skin. Here let me show you."

She then cut open each fruit which had jelly-like segments and large black seeds with a soft off-white skin.

"The skin will get dark when exposed to light."

I watched Nandan bite into the soft fruit. The clear juice ran down his chin and Appu and Thangam laughed to see him juggle the squishy slippery fruit.

"It is so cool and refreshing," he said with amazement in his voice. "We don't get this in Bombay."

"It's grown here in the south," my mother said. "Unfortunately some people use it to make toddy, an alcoholic drink."

Once lunch was over, the twins and I rushed to our house to pack a backpack. We took a spare set of clothes and put on sturdy walking shoes and our jeans. Even though it was warm for long pants, my mother thought we might be glad to have the protection later that night against insect bites. We met with Radha and Jaibal who was going to accompany us. We said good-bye to our guests and followed Kariappan up the slope away from the plantation and into the jungle.

CHAPTER 12
JUNGLE TREK

"How far is your village?" Thangam asked.

"How big is your village and are there many children there?" Appu chimed in.

"I bet it is nice," Thangam added. Neither of them waited for Kariappan to answer.

"Can we reach your village before it gets dark?" Appu asked.

Thangam opened her mouth to ask another question but Kariappan stopped her with a hand gesture. He turned around and looked at them.

"Children, when you walk in the jungle you have to be silent as the panther; otherwise we will miss what is right in front of our eyes. So, walk like a jungle cat, quiet and silent and vigilant. Come follow me."

I had to smile to myself. No one had so effectively put a stop to the twins' chattering. We walked in silence and soon the gentle sounds of the jungle became apparent. The soft drip, drip of moisture as it fell from the leaves onto the ground. The rustle in the bushes as a hidden animal burrowed deeper into the thicket.

"Shhh," Kariappan said. He pointed toward the underbrush.

We had to stare hard because the animals were so cleverly camouflaged in the brush. We stared long and hard before I could make out the shape of a mother deer and her fawns. The two spotted baby deer were lying very close to their mother. The twins exchanged bemused smiles. The scene was so peaceful.

The trees let in very little sunlight and it was dark and damp. The only sound was the deep silence of the woods. Kariappan waved at us and we continued our trek. Much later we arrived at a small stream. Kariappan sat down and removed his sturdy leather sandals. We all sat on the mossy banks.

"Can we drink this water," Thangam whispered.

Kariappan nodded. He dipped his hands in the cool water and drank deeply. I found the water to be refreshing with a pleasant mineral taste. Not as good as Mahagiri water but it was thirst-quenching.

As we trudged deeper into the forest, the air became heavy and moist. We walked up a small slope and came to a stop on the top. I gasped out loud at the breathtaking view of the faraway mountains and the welcome sight of a small but thriving village below us.

Kariappan smiled at the expression on my face. "Beautiful, isn't it?"

I nodded.

"We will live there." He pointed to the houses. "Until the end of the growing season and then we'll move on."

"Why?" Thangam asked.

Kariappan smiled at her.

"We'll talk later, little one. Let's go and wash the dust off our feet."

Even though the village had seemed to be close, it was quite a long walk before we reached the well-trodden path to the village. We were all exhausted after our jungle hike. But Kariappan looked as relaxed as if he had just taken a short stroll in a park. I marveled at his stamina. A few curious children stopped playing in the dirt and stared at us. Thangam and Appu giggled.

"That is my house," said Kariappan, stopping in front of a large hut. "Chella, come meet our guests."

A woman stepped out from the doorway and came toward us. She had gray hair and was dressed in a bright green and yellow sari. Radha went up to her and paid her respects.

"Welcome, Radha. I'm so glad you are here and you brought some friends."

"Yes, Chella aunty," Radha said. "This is my master's daughter Meena and her brother Appu and sister Thangam. This is their driver Jaibal."

I greeted her and thanked her for hosting us. She had many bangles on her brown arms and numerous bead necklaces. They made a pleasing sound when she moved.

"Come you must be tired after all that walking. The sun is setting, so let's get you settled."

She led us to the public tap to wash our feet and hands. We used a small brass pot to clean ourselves. Afterwards, she handed each of us a small cotton towel to dry our face and hands. Radha hung her towel on a clothes line and we all copied her gesture.

"Jaibal, you will sleep with the unmarried men in their dormitory. My husband will be joining you there even though he is not a bachelor." She smiled affectionately at her husband,

"Can I go with Jaibal?" Appu asked.

"Of course," Kariappan said. "You are not married, right?"

Appu giggled, "No. I'm not married. I'm only nine years old."

"Then you are welcome in the bachelors' dormitory."

"What is a bachelors' dormitory," I asked Kariappan.

"The unmarried men live in dormitory style housing. Families have their own huts. In our tribe the men are the most powerful group. They decide disputes, marriage contracts and any other matter," Kariappan explained. "They act as a group so that no one man has absolute power. It is a way to ensure that the young men learn to think as a group or team. They need to learn to work together for the good of the community."

"How long have you lived here?" Radha asked.

"We have lived in this particular village for four years and after this season we will move on."

"Before I met Chella, I had heard only scary stories about the tribal people," Radha said.

"There are a lot of untrue stories about us," Kariappan agreed. "The stories are told by people who have never met us. As you can see we are a peace-loving and independent people. We keep to ourselves and don't interfere with other people."

"I don't think you are scary at all," Thangam said,.

"Sometimes children are wise," Chella said with a smile.

As we talked I noticed that the village was coming to life. Most of the men and women who had gone into the forest for the day were returning with baskets filled with honey combs, dirt-encrusted tubers and roots and fresh fruit.

The five of us were seated close to where wood had been laid out for a bon fire and watched the villagers go to the nearby river to wash up and then gather around the open flames. The bon fire was lit and as the sky darkened and a cool breeze softened the tropical heat, the women came around with serving trays filled with delicacies.

Chella handed us crude wooden plates that had been lined with fresh banana leaves.

"Come eat with us," she urged.

I noticed the villagers used only banana leaves but as honored guests our food was served on wooden plates. There were no other eating utensils. The women used large wooden spoons to serve us mounds of rough red rice smothered in a fiery-hot bean and corn stew. Young girls distributed platters laden with freshly cut pineapple slices, finger-sized yellow and red bananas, and fresh honeycombs dripping golden goodness.

"This is so good," Thangam said, sucking on a honeycomb.

We were handed warm green packages. The green wrapping turned out to be some kind of leaf and inside the tantalizing package was a baked tuber.

"This is a local root that we roast in the fire," Kariappan said. "Try it. It is sweet and filling."

I took a tentative bite of the charred bit of root and found it had a mildly sweet and earthy flavor. It reminded me of a sweet potato and the roasting had enhanced the root's caramelized flavor.

"Is there cinnamon in here?" I asked Chella who had joined us with her banana leaf.

She nodded and swallowed a bite before answering, "Yes, it is cinnamon bark. We throw away the outer bark and use the inner bark for flavoring. You are your father's daughter, Meena, with a taste for spice."

"You said you will leave this area soon. Why?" I asked Kariappan.

"We live in bamboo huts we make ourselves and every day the men and women got out to gather honey, nuts, roots and fruits," Kariappan replied. "We plant several grains and corn and harvest these for no more than five seasons and then we move on."

"That must be hard," I said, thinking of my gypsy friend Priya, "To find a new place to live every few years."

"It is a little hard, but we have learned that if we live in one area for more than five years, the ground becomes fallow and the crops don't grow as well. So we move on to a new area in the forest and there we set fires to the underbrush and use the ashes to fertilize the ground. Since we don't use any kind of chemicals on our crops, we leave the forest as untouched as possible."

Once the main meal was done Chella brought out a plate of nuts, dried raisins and pieces of dried roots. Even though the arrangement didn't look appealing, I was amazed by the flavor and taste of the dried fruits and nuts.

"These are really good," Appu said, grabbing another handful.

"The roots have been soaked in brown sugar or jaggery water and sun-dried," Chella said. "Our children like them too."

"Meena," Radha now spoke up, "did you know they are part of the Muduvan tribe?"

I looked over at Chella who nodded in agreement, "Yes, we use our backs for everything from carrying firewood to sacks of grains to our children. It is our way of life. We use our *mudu* or backs and that is how we got our name."

"Doesn't your back hurt?" Thangam asked.

Chella laughed, "We are used to it, but you need to listen now. That man is Muppan, our tribal elder, and he's going to tell us the story of our people."

"Who is Muppan?" Appu asked.

Chella replied, "He was chosen as the spiritual leader when he was still a young boy. He has sacrificed a lot to be our leader. He has vowed to stay away from women, alcohol and all meat. He performs all the rituals from birth to death."

Now she pointed to a nearby shrine that housed a spear and several sharp bamboo sticks. The shrine was built from woven bamboo mats and a small oil lamp burned at the entrance.

"That is the original way we worshipped. Now if you go to some larger tribes you will see images of gods and goddesses but the original Pandians worshipped Mother Earth. We celebrated her bounty. That shrine stands there because two of our unmarried men were digging in that spot for roots and pulled out a gigantic taro root, so it is a place of good fortune."

"The sticks are our representation of Mother Earth. Every spring, a barren and dry piece of stick comes to life. When the tree is young and growing, it gives us shade, fruit or nuts. When it dies, it provides fuel and firewood.

"The tree is honest truth and positive truth that god is good and benign."

Muppan moved to the center of the circle and the bon fire cast long shadows on everyone. Everyone urged Muppan to tell the story of the tribe.

The twins moved so they were seated on either side of me and I pulled their warm bodies close to mine as we listened to Muppan. He had a huge white moustache that bobbed up and down as he talked. Thangam wanted to laugh each time it moved and I had to poke her ribs and remind her to be quiet, although I could understand her mirth.

"Long ago, when the land was ruled by powerful kings and queens, our people lived in the magnificent city of Madurai. This city was known for its beautiful stone temples. The carvings on the temple walls were said to be so life-like that a young man fell in love with a statue of a beautiful goddess. Our ancestors were peace-loving people and skilled farmers. They were able to coax plants to grow in arid land and soon the fields around the city of Madurai were rich and green.

"But all that prosperity and richness attracted neighboring kings, greedy to share in our city's bounty. There was war, strife and famine. A small group of farmers fled the city and escaped into the jungles. They traveled a long way and found a home here in these forests. These farmers were our ancestors. Since then we don't stay in one place—we live in an area for a few years and then move on. We keep our lands fertile by not over-using them and at the same time we are ready to leave at the first sign of attack."

We had been introduced to another younger man named Mariyappan who now got up and urged the men to dance.

"We must entertain our honored guests," he said.

A group of young men gathered close to the fire and started playing cheerful tunes on crude handmade musical instruments.

The sounds from the guitar, drums and horns were pleasing, if a bit unusual. As the music tempo picked up Muppan got up and started dancing. His steps were methodical and he used his whole body, including his arms which were outstretched as if he were flying. Several other men joined in and soon a group of young boys also started to dance and twirl in the firelight. When the music changed, Mariyappan demonstrated his skills. He twirled, bounced and jumped in a vigorous dance that had the audience clapping along and whistling.

It was late in the evening when Chella led us into her house.

I turned to watch Jaibal along with Kariappan and Appu walk to the men's dormitory.

I found a thick quilt on the floor covered by a heavy, coarse blanket. Radha and Thangam joined me on the floor and we wrapped the blankets around us. I lay awake, listening to the unfamiliar sounds of the village. I could hear the lone hoot of an owl, the shrill cry of a nightingale and the croaks of nearby frogs. Soon even those sounds faded away and as the silence grew deeper, my eyelids began to droop and I finally fell asleep, hugging Thangam close to me.

CHAPTER 13
LEMON PICKLE
AND WHITE RICE

I woke to the sound of roosters heralding the start of a new day. Thangam was still asleep beside me, but Radha's mat was empty. I gently eased out of the blanket and from under Thangam's arm and walked outside. It was early but it was surprisingly light outside and the morning air was cool and refreshing. I found Chella and Radha seated by an open fire, sipping tea. Chella smiled at me and handed me a steel tumbler of hot tea. I took a sip of the liquid, fragrant with cardamom and sweet with wild honey.

Later, Thangam, Appu and Jaibal joined us and we all headed to the river to wash up. The day was warming up and we all enjoyed splashing in the cool river water. I watched as Jaibal dived and swam with the twins. They giggled and splashed. Chella had provided us with rough cotton towels to dry ourselves. We changed into fresh clothes and laid our wet clothes on the huge rocks. The warm sun would dry them in a few hours. We headed back up the gentle slope, ready for breakfast.

Chella showed us how to use twigs to brush our teeth.

"Is that why your teeth are so white?" Appu asked her.

"Yes, we chew on the neem tree leaves and every morning before breakfast I wash my mouth with oil?"

"Eww," Thangam said. "That sounds awful."

Chella smiled, "Not really, I use sesame oil that we make and it is tasty. I hold some in my mouth for a few minutes and then spit it out."

"Why?" I asked her.

"The oil makes my teeth and mouth cleaner. We have been doing this for many, many years and I remember my mother saying that the oil cleaned out your whole body. I don't know how it works but that is our simple belief."

When we reached the village, Kariappan was busy by the open fire. I walked up and saw he was fishing out packets of roasted roots from the embers. The smell of sweet tubers and spice filled the air. Chella opened each leaf package to reveal small tubers, each baked to creamy soft perfection.

Along with the tubers, Chella handed us what looked like bowls made of leaves.

"These are special leaves," she said. "We twist the leaf into a small bowl and use a twig to hold it in place. We use two leaves to make larger bowls."

Each leaf contained a handful of white rice floating in liquid.

"Day old rice that has been soaking in water overnight," Chella said to my unasked question. "The rice stays fresh and cool and is said to settle and soothe upset stomachs. Here, have a bit of lime pickle."

She dropped pieces of a bright yellow and green pickle into my bowl. A few drops of fiery red liquid dripped onto the ground and I noticed the ants scurrying out of the way of the oil. It was probably too spicy even for them. I loved the tantalizing aroma of the pickle.

"These are wild lemons that have a thick skin. I soak them in sesame oil and a paste made from red chilies and spices. I was planning on going into the jungle to gather more. Perhaps you can come with us?"

I nodded as I took a bite of the tangy lemon and pepper pickle. The peel was soft and melted in my mouth. It was a perfect accompaniment to the plain white rice. I followed Kariappan's example and lifted the leafy cup to my mouth and slurped the rest of the liquid and bits of rice.

"That was very good," I said to Chella, who grinned happily at me.

The twins had finished and were watching a group of children playing a complicated game with round river rocks.

I kept an eye on them as I finished the last of my tea. I looked up when Mariyappan came rushing up to the fire.

He addressed Kariappan. "Brother. We have a problem and need to hold a council meeting at once."

Kariappan stood up, a serious expression on his face, "What is the matter? I just came from the dormitory."

"One of the ladies, Swarnamma, says she is missing a pot. It is one she uses to bring water from the river. Last evening before the bon fire and dance, she had gone down to the river and brought it back full of fresh water. She was going to use the water this morning to make tea but when she went to the back of her house where she had stored the pot, it was gone. The pot is not valuable but she is unhappy because of the inconvenience. Now, she is accusing her neighbor of stealing her water pot."

"So who will solve this dispute?" Radha asked. "The young men? What do they know about water and pots?"

I had to agree with her.

"The men are in charge of the smooth running of the place," Kariappan said. "Muppan will preside the meeting. I will be back soon."

While we waited, Radha and I helped Chella clean up.

"I was hoping to air out the blankets and my hut," she said. "Do you want to come with me?"

We went back to her small house. Last night I had not noticed how dark and smoky the interior was but coming in from the bright sunshine, it seemed particularly gloomy this morning. A kerosene lamp in the corner did not do much to brighten the dim interior. It helped a great deal when Chella flung open the windows and propped open the doorway with a stout stick. I could now see that the house had two rooms. The one we entered was clearly a kitchen and dining area. The other room where we had slept was filled with a thick quilt and other beddings, still on the ground. Radha and I helped Chella pick up the blankets and heavy quilt. We took all these outside and draped them over the round rocks in the clearing.

While we waited for the council meeting to finish Radha and I went down to the river and collected our clothes which were now dry. We joined Chella in the shade. Chella chewed on betel nuts while Radha and I peeled and cut some fruit. I worked on some thorny wild pineapples and Radha cut up tiny mangoes. Just then a small boy about five years old ran up to Chella.

"Chella aunty," he said tugging on her sari, "I have something to tell you."

"What is it, Thambi?"

"I can't tell you here. Come with me."

Chella allowed the boy to lead her short distance away from us. The boy talked as Chella listened and then both of them disappeared behind a small hill in the direction of the men's dormitory.

"What do you want to do today, Meena?" Radha asked.

"I would love to stay another night but we told Amma that we would stay for just one day. We should leave today before it gets too dark. What do you think?"

Radha agreed. Soon Kariappan and Chella joined us; they appeared to be in good spirits.

"Was the matter resolved?"

Kariappan chuckled. "It was rather silly. Turns out young Thambi was playing with a ball and accidentally kicked it into the pot which shattered. Instead of telling anyone, he had hidden the pieces in the bushes. He has confessed and the women have forgiven him. They also made peace with each other."

I smiled but had to ask, "Will the boy be punished?"

"Oh yes," Chella's voice was firm. "But it will fit the crime. He has to bring water from the river for both women for a week. It will be hard work but he will learn not to tell lies."

"That is a fair and just way of dealing with the issue," I said. "It is almost something that my mother would do."

Chella looked at me, "Your mother sounds like a wise woman."

She turned to her husband, "Perhaps when you walk our guests back to their home, I can come too? I would like to meet Meena's mother."

"Of course," Kariappan said. He then looked at me, "So, Meena when would you like to return home. You are welcome to stay as long as you wish."

"Radha and I were just talking about that Kariappan uncle," I said. "I would like to return this evening if that is convenient for you."

"Of course," he said. "But I think Chella wants to show you our jungle and where the lemon trees grow."

I remembered that she had invited us to go lemon picking in the jungle.

"I look forward to that."

Radha and Jaibal stayed back to watch over Thangam and Appu, who wanted to play with the village children. So I set off to pick lemons with Chella, Mariyappan and Kariappan.

"All this used to be jungle," Kariappan pointed out. "We cleared the brush and we are barely holding the jungle back. We approach the jungle as if we are peeling an onion or fruit. We take each layer away until we are left with a patch of earth. We carefully trim the larger trees and branches. We pull the weeds and clear the underbrush. If the underbrush is too thick, we burn it to provide ash for our fields. We only clear space we need. We respect Mother Earth."

I could see where the jungle was slowly encroaching on the village. The vines, creepers and bushes were growing thicker each year and as soon as Kariappan and his villagers left this place, it would soon return to its original glory. The villagers' method of farming really was a better way to take care of the earth. I made a mental note of this to share with my mother. She would find it interesting.

I followed Kariappan. Chella was right behind me with an empty basket on her head. I carried a smaller basket. The morning coolness had long since vanished. It was hot and humid under the trees. Kariappan seemed to know the way and I mindlessly followed him deep into the woods.

"There," he pointed.

I looked in the direction he was pointing and noticed a tree studded with bright yellow fruit. The tree was tucked away among the shrubs and I didn't think I would have seen it at first glance.

Soon we were twisting off the citrus fruit and the air was filled with their fresh scent.

"Meena, if you can reach, can you gather some tender leaves? They make the best chutney."

The sharp clean tang of lemon and lemon leaves was a heady scent. Soon our baskets were full and we headed up the hill back to the village.

We were greeted by the twins who were happy to see me.

"Chechi, we learned a new game today," Thangam said. "Watch me."

She showed me a game where she used a larger rock to move a row of smaller stones. Each time she hit and moved a smaller rock she gained a point. Jaibal got up to greet me.

"Are we are leaving today?" he asked. I nodded but before I could reply I could hear Chella calling my name.

"Come on, Meena. Help me with the chutney."

I hurried over to where she and Radha were washing and drying the lemons, I said over my shoulder, "We'll leave after our mid-day meal Jaibal."

"We'll pickle some of the lemons," Chella said as I joined her. "Meena, you can peel the fruit. We'll save a few to use for a drink. The children love lemon water sweetened with honey."

I carefully peeled the lemons using a sharp knife, avoiding the bitter white pith. While I was busy peeling the lemons, Chella had fried some dal, spices and fiery hot dried red peppers in an iron skillet. She added the peels to the dal and spices. Using a stone mortar and pestle she started to crush the mixture. Radha asked to take over and worked on getting the chutney to a smooth consistency.

Meanwhile, Chella mixed some flour and water in a wooden bowl.

"What are you making?" I asked.

"This is chickpea flour. I'm adding salt and some dried herbs and a bit of coconut oil," she said. "Then I'll make pancakes or dosas with the batter."

Soon she had thin crepes cooking in an iron frying pan. The toasted coconut oil and chickpea flour gave off a tantalizing aroma. We all gathered around the fire watching Chella prepare the crepes.

When I finally tasted the delicate crepes filled with tangy lemon peel chutney, I knew the wait was worth it. Each bite of citrusy spicy hot chutney was wrapped in a soft crepe flavored with the delicate taste of chickpeas.

"This is the best lemon drink," Thangam said, taking another gulp.

"I'm glad you like it, little one. It has wild honey and fresh lemons your sister picked this morning."

After our meal, we packed our clothes and said our goodbyes to the villagers, many of whom had gathered to see us off. This time Chella accompanied us and we were soon walking down the path away from the tiny village.

On the way we stopped to watch a herd of water buffalo. A large bull stood guard, watching his herd nibble on tufts of grass. The buffalo herd was too busy eating to notice us and we walked around the clearing to avoid disturbing them.

When we reached the hillside overlooking my father's plantation, I stopped and showed the view to the twins.

"This is our father's place," I told them, gesturing to the land below us.

It was getting dark by the time we reached our farm and I was glad to see my mother.

"Amma, this is Chella aunty," I said pulling Chella forward. "She took good care of us and wanted to meet you."

My mother greeted Chella and took her to the kitchen for a warm drink.

"Meena, Thangam, Appu you go take a hot bath while I visit with Chella," she said on her way to the kitchen.

I waited until the twins were done and then hurriedly washed the dirt off my feet and hair. I was eager to join everyone on the veranda.

My mother smiled at me, "I was just sharing with Chella Nandan's plan for the estate. They agree it is a good one. I think your father would have been pleased."

After a meal of whole wheat bread and potatoes, I left Chella, Paru Amma and my mother in the kitchen and wandered through the front yard of my father's estate. I could hear the cicadas singing and the frogs croaking. It was a warm night and the sky was lit with a thousand little points of lights, stars twinkling as if their life depended on it. I walked by the vanilla bean creeper, its vines heavy with long beans. The smooth beans were cool to touch. I continued to the front porch of the farmstead and sat down to wait for my mother.

CHAPTER 14
PILGRIMAGE

THE LEGEND OF LORD AYAPPAN

Long ago there was a demon named Mahishi and like most demons she had received a boon from the gods and so she could not be killed by anyone but a child of Lord Shiva and Lord Vishu. The demon thought she was indestructible. To save the world from her, Lord Vishu took the form of Mohini, a beautiful maiden, and seduced Lord Shiva. Mohini gave birth to a baby boy named Ayappan. The boy was left on the banks of the Pampa River where King Rajashekhara of Pandalam found him and later adopted him as his own son. Soon after the king adopted Ayyappan, his queen gave birth to a son, Raja Rajan. Both boys grew up together and Ayappan was known for his intelligence, strength and knowledge of the scriptures as well as weaponry. Even his "guru" knew he was superhuman and asked for his blessing instead of a -"teacher fee"- at the end of his training. According to legend, Ayyappan blessed his guru's son who was both blind and mute and healed him.

The king had chosen Ayyappa to be his heir but the queen wanted her own son to be crowned king so she pretended to fall ill. She conspired with her physician and the king's minister to kill Ayyappan. The physician told the king the only remedy for the queen's illness was milk from a lactating tigress. Ayyappan was the only one who volunteered to bring the milk to cure the queen. On the way he came across the demon Mahishi and killed her on the banks of the River Azhutha. When Ayyappan entered the forest,

*he was met by Lord Shiva who blessed him. So Ayappan returned
to the kingdom, riding on the back of a tigress.*

*The king heard about his queen's betrayal and begged Ayappan
for forgiveness. The lord forgave the king and asked him to build a
temple in his name in Sabarimala. Lord Ayappan then returned
to his heavenly abode.*

*Each year thousands of pilgrims visit Lord Ayappan's temple
during the winter months.*

—~*As re-told by Sudha*

The next morning Mac and Nandan came for a late
breakfast. Over coconut filled crepes I told them about my trip
to the tribal village. Chella and Kariappan took their leave after
breakfast.

"Promise you'll never forget us," Chella said to me.

"I'm sure she will be visiting this place again," Nandan
assured her. "You are welcome and so are Meena and her family."

Meanwhile a couple of the laborers had come to the edge of
the veranda, trying to get my mother's attention. I noticed they
were all dressed in black and had heavy beards. My mother
walked down the steps and spoke with them. They bowed with
folded palms and soon left.

"What was that all about?" I asked.

"Didn't you notice they were dressed to go to the Ayyappan
temple?"

I replied, "Oh, so that's why they were in black."

In Mahagiri I had seen the men dressed in black, unshaven
with prayer beads around their necks, but had never really paid
any attention to them.

"They are leaving tonight to go to Sabarimala and want us
to come to the temple to send them off."

My mother looked at me, "You know the rules about going
to the Ayappan temple?"

"Not all of them. I know they wear black and don't shave."

"Well," my mother said, "when they take on the beads they are asked to follow a very strict regimen for forty one days. They need to bathe twice a day, repeat their prayers and eat special foods. They also have to sleep on the floor and stay away from women, including menstruating girls."

"Lord Ayyappan was sure tough to please," I joked.

But my mother didn't laugh. "Meena, it is no laughing matter. These men take their devotions to the lord very seriously. We are invited to the temple for a special pooja where we will send them off on their way to see Lord Ayyappan and climb the sacred eighteen steps to his temple."

I was eager to go to the ceremony but later that day I started my menses and my mother told me stay home. I felt a little put out and lonely until Nandan and Mac showed up for a surprise visit. We sat on the porch and drank cups of cardamom tea and snacked on cashews and banana chips.

"You know, Meena," Nandan said, sitting back in this chair, "you should study agricultural business in college. Mac has told me you are interested in plants and growing things."

I nodded, "I am. I guess I've always been around gardens and plants. I had thought about that but my uncle didn't think it was a suitable major for a young girl. He thinks I should look at a career as a bank teller."

"I think he may be wrong. Girls do a lot of things now. One of my daughters is a doctor and the other one wants to go into architecture. She has been interested in this since she visited my building sites as a young girl," he laughed.

"You don't mind that?"

"No, I want them to be independent and take care of themselves. Their brother will look out for them, of course, but it is the girls' responsibility to take care of their own needs."

I was taken aback at this.

"I think running a farm would be respectable," Nandan said. "Your mother does it."

It was true my mother had been a business woman for a long time and no one thought less of her.

"You have given me an idea," I said. "I think I'll look into that when I go to California."

"When will that be?" Mac asked.

I shrugged my shoulder. "I'm not sure. I'm hoping soon."

My mother returned later that evening and the twins were bursting with stories about the temple ceremony.

"They carried yellow cloth bags as a symbol of their pilgrimage," Thangam said.

I had no idea what she was talking about and looked at my mother. I was starting to feel a little annoyed I had to be left out of these rituals.

"She's talking about the *Irumudi Kettu* which is a bundle carried on the head. All devotees must have the *Irumudi* on the head to enter the temple grounds and walk up the sacred eighteen steps."

I was reluctant to show any interest in the proceedings that excluded me and asked rather grudgingly, "What's in the *Irumudi*?"

"There are two punches in each *Irumudi* and the temple priests help fill them. They draw the symbol for Om on the front pouch and fill it with items for conducting *pooja* such as coconuts, ghee, rice, fruit, sandalwood paste, incense sticks, holy ashes, candied sugar and coins.

"The rear pouch of the *Irumudi Kettu* is sort of a suitcase containing the personal items the pilgrim needs for his journey."

My mother then went on to explain that everything a devotee needs has to be carried on his head, including his bedding."

"And just before they left they broke a coconut on the stone steps of the temple and we chanted 'Saranam Ayyappa,'" Appu said.

"The coconut is broken at the beginning and end of the journey," my mother added.

Thangam had the last word, "It was so much fun, Chechi. You should have been there."

Before going to bed I stopped by the large colorful artist's rendering of Lord Ayappan. He looked so benevolent on top of a fierce tigress. Why would such a kindly looking god ban women from his temple? I couldn't help feeling a little let down by Lord Ayyappan. I sighed and reached out and touched his perfect feet with my fingers. *You may have banned me from your temple but I will still pray to you and ask your blessings.*

CHAPTER 15
HERE AND GONE

The trip was bittersweet one as we said good-bye to my father's plantation. Even though we made promises to return, I knew in my heart of hearts I would not be going back. My home was in Mahagiri. And I now was back here, trying to cram one last saree into my bulging suitcase.

A journey doesn't begin with the first step; it begins with a stuffed suitcase and ends with a frustrated packer. I sat back on my heels for a moment and stared at my suitcases. I couldn't believe I was finally on my way to America.

The days after our trip to Chandur had flown by. I had been busy with paperwork and then packing. Finally everything was in order and I was going to be on a plane tomorrow night. After packing, I spent the day wandering the gardens, the orchards, all the rooms in our house and finally the kitchen. I touched a smoky wall, my fingers lingering. Now that it was time to leave, I found I wanted to stay within these walls. What was wrong with me? I had visited Mac and said my good-byes.

"Now, lass, four years will pass before you know it and you'll be back here drinking tea and telling me American stories."

I nodded and blinked back tears.

"And be sure to write. Write long letters," Mac said.

I promised and now I had the painful task of saying good-bye to Thangam and Appu. They clung to me and we all sobbed.

My mother finally pulled us apart. "Come now. Your sister is going to college. This is a celebration, not a funeral."

"Little Mother," Jaibal was at the door.

"Yes?" My mother walked into the hallway to talk to him. I followed, curious at Jaibal's panicked look.

"Did you look at your ticket, Meena?"

I shook my head, "No. I glanced at it. I mean, I didn't study it or anything."

"Well, look carefully at the time of departure."

I took the airline ticket he held out to me and looked closely at the date and time.

"Oh no," I said. "It says 12 a.m. tonight, not tomorrow night."

We had reservations on the early morning train from Pellaur to Madras which would get us in plenty of time for the night plane. Or we thought.

Suddenly all my doubts vanished and I couldn't imagine missing that plane. I wanted to weep with anger.

"How could I have been so stupid," I wailed.

"Meena, it's alright. Jaibal, we are going to hire you to take her to Madras. If you start driving now, you should make it by tonight."

She turned to me and took my face in her hands.

"You will make that plane. I will come with you and make sure."

So before I knew it, my mother and I were in the back seat of Jaibal's taxi and we were leaving. The next few hours were hard. We stopped to take only one break and poor Jaibal drove like a madman, avoiding busy streets and finding frontage roads. We whizzed past small villages, large towns and one huge city. Everything was a blur. I sat in the backseat with my foot pressed down on the floor, as if I could make the car go faster.

It was late evening when we finally entered the city. Traffic was slow and I was glad to see signs for the airport. We had arrived, with just an hour to spare. There was no time for tears or long good-byes. Before I knew it, I was waving to my mother through a thick Plexiglas window. *Good bye, Amma.*

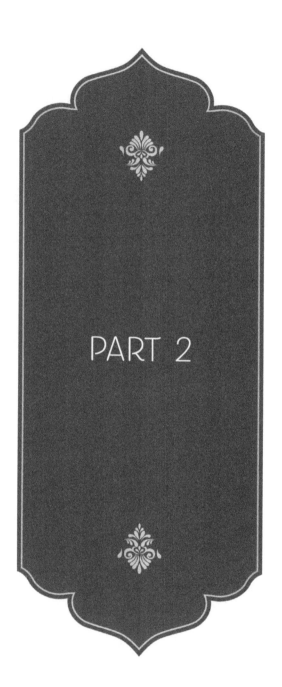

PART 2

CHAPTER 16
ARRIVING

The airport was vibrating with emotion like a tuning fork. All the hellos and goodbyes seemed to have seeped into the waiting room. I shifted my heavy shoulder bag and scanned the lobby, looking for a familiar face.

"Hey, little cousin," a voice called out. "Meena, here I am!"

It was my cousin Chitra. She pulled me into her arms for a very enthusiastic and non-Indian greeting.

"Sorry Mum and Dad couldn't come," she said. "Let's go pick up your bags and get out of this place."

Before I knew it we were in her little Toyota sedan.

"Buckle your seatbelt," she said, looking in the rearview mirror as she pulled into the busy traffic.

And just like that I was in America.

CHAPTER 17
COLLEGE

My time with my uncle Ramanunny or Unny and my aunt Malathi was exciting and challenging. Chitra and her family lived in the small northern California town of Santarem named after Saint Irene of Portugal and pronounced *Santa Ream*. Over the years I would learn that the university was named after the saint and the town after the city in Portugal that was re-named to honor the saint after her death. Unlike other towns up and down the coast there was no mission or real tourist attraction beyond the spectacular coastline and the well-known college. The main drag sported antique stores, cafes, restaurants and clothing boutiques.

Chitra was a political science major, hoping to go to law school. She was also very active on the campus. I started out as a biology major, but with Nandan's advice in mind I had changed it to an independent study major focusing on farming and agriculture classes. I absorbed all the latest information about irrigation, soil science and pest control and couldn't wait to share all this with my mother and Bhojan. I imagined how impressed Mac would be with my knowledge. I wrote long letters to my mother, the twins and Mac.

It was a tumultuous time on campus with sit-ins and shouting over the college's investments in South Africa. I longed to join Chitra on the quad but my uncle warned me to stay away from the demonstrations.

"Meena, you are here on a student visa. Don't do anything to jeopardize it," he said.

So I hung out on the edges of the crowds, watching Chitra on the microphone, urging students to walk out of classrooms and write letters to the college president. Even when she was threatened with arrest, Chitra was defiant and refused to back down. Thanks in part to her persistent efforts; the college did eventually withdraw its investments.

Because I missed my mother and her kitchen, I started to spend time with my aunt Malathi, a kind and gentle woman who thought the world was changing too rapidly. She was old-school, having grown up in a traditional Hindu family in south India. She tried her best to keep those traditions alive. She was the most open-minded in the kitchen, willing to experiment with new flavors and cooking methods. Even though she had been brought up vegetarian, she learned to use eggs to make cakes and cookies.

"Sometimes we have to change, Meena," she would say, "Otherwise, how are you going to learn?"

Even though she had a difficult time watching her daughter become so vocal in campus politics, she never criticized her choices. I found solace and companionship in her kitchen. My aunt's California kitchen was open and airy with modern appliances, so very different from the smoky cozy one in Mahagiri. Under my aunt's tutelage I found myself tasting and cooking with different ingredients and interesting vegetables.

"The key to cooking with fresh vegetables," Malathi would say "is to never overcook them."

I watched as she grated a potato, a beet and an onion. She mixed these together with an egg, a pinch of salt and some fresh herbs.

"You cook these cakes on a hot griddle, instead of frying them," she said as the kitchen filled with the delicious aroma of the crispy cakes.

My aunt had a sophisticated palate and I learned to use different herbs to add flavor and depth to food. She enjoyed a vast variety of cheeses and soon I could distinguish the salty tang of feta cheese, the sharp bite of yellow cheddar and the mild sweetness of fresh ricotta. I collected dozens of new recipes which I was eager to share with Devi and my mother. While on campus I joined the Film Club and every Wednesday afternoon, I would walk into Clements Hall on campus with my brown bag lunch to lose myself in movies such as *Chinatown*, *The Maltese Falcon and Citizen Kane*. My world was expanding.

The campus was beautiful and I especially enjoyed the library. I loved walking up the stairs and finding a nook to sit and study. Once in a while I would stand by one of the expansive windows and look down onto the greens. Young men, shirtless and tanned, could be seen throwing Frisbees, while others were kicking around a soccer ball. I could see young couples sitting together, heads bent close, consulting notes or kissing passionately. It was a life that was just beyond my fingertips! I am not sure whether I wanted to be a part of it or not but the sight of the kissing couples left me with a strange ache in my heart.

My mother had agreed to let me stay with my uncle Ramanunny confident that I would be well looked after. He and aunty Malathi took that task to heart. The town was so small that the college was within walking distance of my uncle's house. Every morning I would set out along a small dirt path that led down from the house to the university. The view was beautiful with the ocean on one side and tidy little cottages on the other.

I enjoyed the walk and the freedom. The cool sea breeze carried a salty tang, so different from the mountain air of my hometown. The days flew by, seasons changed and before I knew it I had been in California for three years.

CHAPTER 18
BIRTHDAY BASH

Chitra could always be counted on to bring a bit of adventure and new experiences into my life. For my 21st birthday, she insisted on taking me wine tasting. Santarem had no local wineries but we weren't far from the famous Napa Valley. My uncle, who loved a glass of good wine with his meal, was agreeable and volunteered to drive us. I had no idea that pairing fermented grape juice with cheese or even chocolate could set off an explosion of flavors in my mouth.

When we returned from that trip, I felt a little giddy and lightheaded and it wasn't all from the alcohol. The idea that wine could be paired with food to bring out the best flavors in both was such an intriguing.

My aunt, who never drank wine, indulged me and soon I was finding ways to pair wine with food. Under her guidance, I roasted vegetables and then layered them between soft lasagna noodles. Fresh cracked walnuts, ricotta cheese and a homemade tomato sauce finished the dish. My uncle helped choose the right red to bring out the bold flavors of the roasted root vegetables and the rich red sauce.

Would it be possible to grow grapes in Mahagiri? When I mentioned this to my aunt, she shook her head, "Meena, I don't think it would be easy to grow wine grapes in Mahagiri but I have another idea for you. Tomorrow afternoon you and I will go out."

I wondered what my aunt had planned for us.

CHAPTER 19
TEA TIME

"This place has a lot of different kinds of tea," said Aunty Malathi, as she led me into the tea shop. The shop was located off Main Street its unprepossessing entrance in stark contrast to what was behind the door. A waitress wearing a black apron bowed and led us through the shop to the back. I stopped in my tracks at the sight of the lush scene before me.

"Welcome to the House of Tea," the waitress said, smiling at the astonished look on my face. "This is your first time here?"

I nodded, letting my eyes take in the beauty before me.

"Then let me tell you about our traditions."

Unlike a regular restaurant, here the waitress was also the mistress of the tea ceremony and part to her job was to educate the customer. As she walked us down the pebbled path, she told us the story of how tea came to China.

"Once upon a time, nearly 3,000 years before Jesus Christ was born, Emperor Shen Nung ruled China. One day he was tired after walking and decided to rest under a tree. He had his servants set up camp under the tree and instructed one of his men to start a fire and boil some water. The careless manservant didn't notice a few leaves from the tree had dropped into the boiling water. He pulled the leaves out before handing a cup of the hot liquid to the emperor who liked the taste of the hot water so much that the servant confessed about finding the leaves floating in the boiling water. The tree under which Emperor Shen Nung had stopped was a wild tea tree. And so the tradition of tea drinking was born."

"She has never seen a tea ceremony," my aunt told the waitress. "What is your specialty today?"

"Today we serve Chinese oolong tea," she said. "I will be back with your tea. Please enjoy your surroundings."

I looked around the quiet garden. I felt as I had just walked into a peaceful oasis. The street noises were faint in here among the lush trees, bushes and flowers. We were seated at a low wooden table with benches on either side. The bench was covered with a thick cushion embroidered with a green and red dragon. The waitress came back with placemats, bamboo spoons and delicate tea cups. She placed these in a very precise manner on the table, adjusting each item until it was in the spot she wanted. This took quite a while. Chinese tea ceremony was not to be hurried.

"We are performing the gungfu tea ceremony at our tea house," she said. "Everything is done in a precise manner. We use traditional Chinese tea which is stored in this bamboo canister."

She used bamboo spoons to measure out the tea into strange shaped tea pots.

"This tea pot is a Yixing pot made from fine porcelain. It complements the black tea. In China black tea is called red tea and you'll see why when I pour the tea into these white cups."

"Is there a reason everything is placed in such a precise way?" I asked.

"There is a special place for each tool," the waitress replied to my question. "The water is just boiled and then added to the special blend of oolong tea."

As the steam rose from the small tea pot, I could smell the delicate fragrance of the seeping leaves. While the leaves were seeping, another waitress brought over a tray with different kinds of baked and fried wonton rolls.

"You requested the vegetarian rolls?" she asked. "Since our dumplings are not vegetarian, I've brought you wonton rolls. We call them dumplings even though they are not the traditional dumpling we serve."

My aunt nodded and turned to me, "I tasted these snacks for the first time with your uncle. We tried the eggplant and ginger rolls."

"Today we have three varieties of dumplings," waitress laid out the small snack, each one was glistening and ready to burst. "The first one is a garlicky greens dumpling. We also have eggplant and ginger dumpling and for a sweet we have apricot orange dumplings."

She laid out the wontons on delicate porcelain plates using bamboo chopsticks.

"Have a sip of tea before you eat," she instructed us. "Cleanse your palate."

The tea did look red as she poured us each a cup. There was no sugar or milk in this brew. I blew on the surface and tentatively took a sip. I was surprised by the floral and fragrant taste.

"This is very different from Indian chai," I said.

My aunt nodded and the waitress beamed at us. "Yes, Indian spice tea is good but this is very different and good for your digestion and health."

It was peaceful in this garden tea house. In the distance I could hear the faint sound of water splashing. I looked over my aunt's shoulder at a mini-fountain with a water wheel. I sipped the hot tea and munched on the dumplings. I almost mastered the chopsticks until a dumpling plopped out and fell to the ground. The apricot dumpling, sweet and tangy, was my favorite.

"Can't you see such a tea ceremony being popular in Mahagiri?" asked my aunt as we made our way out of the peaceful garden. I nodded and said, "You are right, Aunty. Not only are the tea and snacks delicious I like the idea of sitting down and enjoying a leisurely cup of tea. I will have to learn the ceremony. It seems like it is very precise."

"It is," said my aunt, "I think there are some classes on tea ceremonies at the university's cultural center."

That fall I enrolled in a tea gathering seminar and in a soil and agricultural classes devoted to terraced gardening. I had to smile as I imagined Muthi sitting down to a cup of tea that had no sugar or milk. But I knew Mac would be intrigued by this ceremony. I remembered him saying he was experimenting with different kinds of tea in his greenhouse. Had he mentioned Chinese?

CHAPTER 20
A JAPANESE TEA GATHERING

It was my final year at university, but I was constantly discovering new things to do on campus. I had no idea the university had a Japanese tea garden until I saw a flyer advertising a Japanese-style tea gathering. I followed the directions and walked down a set of broad concrete steps and found myself in the tidiest garden I had ever seen. Several trees were planted in strategic spots to give shade and add green tranquility to the space. The red leaves of the maple trees formed a dramatic backdrop to the lone pine standing guard at the entrance of the garden. There were several wooden benches. I stood still and listened to the gentle sound of running water. A miniature Japanese water wheel was turning slowly and methodically in a corner of the garden. It was a hypnotic and soothing sound. I sat down on one of the rough wooden benches and listened to the peaceful sound of water and chirping birds. I felt I was far away from the university, even though the main quad was just a few feet away.

A gentle voice roused me. "Excuse me; are you here for the tea gathering?"

I opened my eyes to see a petite, gray-haired Japanese woman wearing a dark red wine-colored kimono. For a moment I thought I was in Japan.

I stood up. "Yes, I am. I got caught up in the beauty of this garden and lost track of time. I'm sorry."

"No need to apologize. Please come take a seat."

I followed her into a large conference room with a raised platform on one end, sort of like a stage. A large panel with beautiful calligraphy writing hung in the alcove on one side of the stage. A half-opened pink flower added a splash of color. There was a low table with cushions in the center of the platform. The room started to fill up as students entered and found seats on folding chairs. I found a spot near the front and tucked my bag under the chair.

The woman spoke in such a quiet and gentle voice that I had to concentrate to catch every word.

"Long ago in Japan when the Lord Buddha wandered the countryside in one of his incarnations he was known as the Dharma. This incarnation of Lord Buddha was very hard on himself, continuously sitting for long hours of meditation trying to stay awake. But he often found that after walking for miles he was tired and when he tried to meditate, he fell asleep. Furious with himself, he cut off his eyelashes and threw them down on the ground. Years later he came back to the same place and found a bush had grown where his eyelashes had landed. The villagers brewed the leaves from this bush to stay alert. Soon it became a tradition to plant tea bushes wherever the Dharma visited. There were hundreds of bushes and villagers used the brew for vigor and health."

The next hour flew by as I watched a woman, dressed in traditional Japanese robes, prepare green tea.

"Listen," she said.

We sat quietly but heard nothing for a moment. Then I thought I heard a soft squishing sound.

"That is the sound of wind through the pines," she said with a smile. "That means the water is boiling and ready to be poured into the tea pot."

Even the napkin had to be folded in a precise way, dictated by age-old custom.

"We shake the dust off the world when we enter this room and enjoy our tea," said the hostess as she prepared to pour cups of green tea.

Each of us was given a thin wafer, a kind of sweet biscuit and then bowls of warm green tea. The tea was very different from Indian or even Chinese tea. It was thick, almost grassy in taste.

"Enjoy every drop and slurp it up," said the hostess. "It is impolite to leave any tea in the bowl."

There was a feeling of timelessness in that modern conference room. I felt my body and mind slowing down as I slurped the last few drops. The sweet wafer added the right amount of sweetness to the grassy tea. The after-taste was soothing and pleasant.

"In a proper Japanese tea gathering," said the hostess, "it would take up to seven hours to complete the ceremony and by then the beautiful flower in the alcove would have shed its petals. If the hostess timed the ceremony perfectly, the last of the petals would drop as the guests put down their tea bowls."

I planned to visit this garden again to learn more about the Japanese way of drinking tea.

CHAPTER 21
A NEW YORK, NY

In my final year of college, my uncle generously offered to fly me to visit my friend Kumari in New York where she was pursuing a degree in theater.

The flight from the west coast to the east coast was long but nothing like the tedious one from India. A dentist, next to me, was very talkative about himself revealing bits of information about his divorce that I really didn't want to hear. He was also very enthusiastic about flossing and made me promise to floss every day.

I was glad when the plane landed in New York and I saw Kumari's smiling face. She was waiting for me near the baggage claim area. New York was very different from the quiet and quaint little town of Santarem. The incessant city noises and crowded sidewalks were overwhelming. I was thankful that Kumari was with me because I would have been lost in seconds. We took a taxi to her small apartment in an area she called the Village, though it looked nothing like what we called a village in India.

"I'm just sub-letting this place while the owner is abroad," she explained. The tiny apartment was charming.

That weekend we walked all over the city, like tourists. When we tired of walking we rode the famous subway trains from station to station. One of my favorite spots was the green and quirky Central Park.

"This reminds me of Governor's Park," I told Kumari, who looked a little dubious.

"No jugglers in that park," she said. "Besides, Central Park is kind of open and filled with musicians and street performers. Our botanical garden is laid out very precisely and people can't wander in without buying a ticket."

I couldn't argue with that but somehow the green space and trees reminded me of my own hometown.

"I really miss Mahagiri," I told Kumari that night as we feasted on chewy and flavorful New York style pizza.

It was the most delicious pizza I had ever tasted.

"I'll never be able to eat any other kind of pizza," I said, swallowing the last bite of crust.

"So you are going back?" asked Kumari, bringing the conversation back to Mahagiri.

I nodded and took a sip of the rough red wine. "Yes. Uncle Unny was happy to help me look for a job in Santarem but I miss Mahagiri, my mom and the twins. I can't imagine living anywhere else."

"Well it is the opposite for me," Kumari confided. "I'm so happy in New York."

"Don't you get lonely?"

"Not really. I'm really busy with the theater."

Kumari had become fascinated with theater production and now volunteered at a local theatre.

"It's all volunteer time right now," she said, "But soon I'll get paid and until then my parents are helping me out."

The only condition, she said, was they were going to arrange her marriage.

"As long as it someone who lives in New York and will let me work, I'm happy. What about you, Meena?"

I shrugged, "I don't exactly know but like you it will have to be someone who wants to live in Mahagiri."

"Perhaps you'll find a nice Badaga boy," Kumari teased. The local tribes belonged to the Badaga clan and they were known for keeping a distance from most of the Mahagiri residents. They considered us newcomers. Our cowhands Bhojan and Raman belonged to a local Badaga tribe.

"I doubt they'll want me as a daughter-in-law," I said, giggling at the idea. "They would say I was such a wimp."

Badaga women were known for working alongside their husbands, laboring in the fields and orchards. There were stories of the women pausing to give birth while working in the potato fields.

"Can you imagine me giving birth and then going back to working?" I asked.

"No," Kumari giggled, "Besides, your mother would be right there."

I realized she was right. My mother would be right alongside me. Living in Mahagiri was a great dream but it would mean always being a daughter. Perhaps I would have to re-think my future plans, but not now. Tonight I was going to make an Indian meal for Kumari. My mother's famous lemon rice with a coconut ginger stew which I spiked with tender pieces of purple Russian kale.

"Who would have thought kale would be good in ishtu?" said Kumari, as she spooned the creamy stew onto a mound of tangy yellow rice. "You certainly are a good cook, Meena. I miss coming to your house for meals."

"I always thought my mother was a good cook," I replied. "And her Indian dishes are the best, but my aunt Malathi is so inventive. She takes traditional Indian recipes and mixes them with California vegetables to create the most amazing dishes. I love her Quinoa uppma."

For dessert I had made my aunt's— "chocolate mousse"— which was a rich creamy and incredibly decadent. The little Korean market close to Kumari's flat had bags of tiny tangerines called "pages" and I served the chocolate mousse with slices of juicy tangerine bits.

"Oh," Kumari said after the first mouthful of chocolate and tangerine. "This is the best dessert ever. You should become a chef."

The next morning I took a taxi back to the airport. We hugged each other good-bye, promising to visit and write.

"You brought a bit of Mahagiri to New York," Kumari said. "I bet you will be a business tycoon with world-class tea-tasting room in Mahagiri."

I returned her hug, "Come visit me. I don't know about being a business tycoon but I'm going to try and convince my mom to give me a chance to serve different kinds of tea in Mahagiri."

CHAPTER 22
HEADING HOME

After my visit with Kumari, time seemed to fly by, and before I knew it graduation was over. Chitra was busy with law school applications and so we said our goodbyes at a graduation party held at a local restaurant. In my four years of schooling in California I had gained a healthy respect for farming. One of the highlights had been helping out at the university's small farm. In an almost forgotten corner of the university, a group of volunteers worked hard to produce greens, tomatoes and melons. The farm had help from the college agricultural program and was now on the verge of expanding. So I had spent many a hot afternoon digging, weeding and planting. I loved harvesting because it was so satisfying to hold in your hands what you helped plant. The college had a small grove of pomegranate trees and residents were invited to tour the orchard and farm. Santarem residents came with bags and filled them with the fruit and greens. There was music and food and it was like a huge party for the community. Even though I loved every moment of my time in the California sunshine, I was starting to miss my hilltop home. I missed Mahagiri with an intensity that surprised me. I remembered how much I had wanted to leave that place four years ago. Now, all I wanted was to return home. Some nights I woke up with an empty heart and a feeling of loss. My aunt was hoping I would settle down in California but I knew my future lay in Mahagiri.

Once our celebration ended, I was ready to go home. Soon I was at the airport, waiting in line to check-in my baggage.

Crying babies, old men and women and Indian businessmen all stood patiently like a herd of cattle on market day. I used my feet to push my suitcase along as the line crept up to the check-in counter.

When I got rid of my suitcase and received my boarding pass it was time to go stand in another line. This one was even slower but finally it was my turn. The TSA worker was a young African American woman who looked a little bored with the process. But something about me must have piqued her interest because she perked up when she saw. She asked me to step aside and waved a metal wand up my front side and then my back side. She asked me to raise my arms to make sure I wasn't smuggling anything under my armpits. Finally she allowed me to go through the security gates and I boarded the bus to the plane. The bus was crowded and I hung onto the large plastic straps for dear life as it bounced across the tarmac to the waiting plane.

It was warm and noisy in the confines of the cabin. I held my carry-on backpack in front of me and tried to walk around passengers stuffing the overhead compartments with their luggage. The flight was going to Singapore with a re-fueling stop in Hawaii. It was crammed with vacation goers as well as Indians on their way to Singapore and beyond. I found my seat number, a window seat I had requested. At the moment the other two seats in my row were empty. I stored my backpack under the seat, sat down, buckled up and turned the overhead nozzle control to get more air flowing.

My eventual seatmate was a young Chinese fellow who after nodding at me buried his face in a Chinese language newspaper. We took off without incident and a little while later drinks were served and then dinner which filled the airplane with a tangle of aromas, a veritable battlefield of scents. The air was heavy with the scents of meat, spicy Indian food, overcooked vegetables and sweaty human beings. You really need an iron stomach to travel in a confined airplane because the odors alone could make you gag.

After dinner service, the lights were dimmed and we watched a movie. Michael J. Fox's face popped up on the screen and we were on a crazy ride *"Back to the Future."* The movie was very entertaining and I enjoyed it a great deal. With perhaps a couple of hours left in the flight, I decided to get some rest. It seemed like I'd just fallen asleep when the lights came back on. Apparently it was time for breakfast.

I had chosen a window seat thinking I could pass the time looking out at the view. But I had forgotten that a plane was not a train and there was nothing to see. Outside my tiny window there was only a black void, no quaint stations bustling with life and lights. Hour after hour of blank darkness was not a good view. I made a mental note to ask for an aisle seat in the future.

The plane landed with a tiny bump and all the tourists were eager to get out and start their vacations. I waited for the first rush to be over before getting up. Since there was more than an hour before we took off for Singapore, I decided to take this opportunity to stretch my legs. The Chinese man— his name was Han Soo— followed me down the ramp. The air in the covered ramp was moist and warm but soon we were back in air-conditioned comfort. I preferred the fresh air to this recycled airplane air. Some things should not be re-used!

Honolulu airport was large, clean and filled with Hawaiian themes. I loved the tropical flower patterns. Han Soo smiled and bowed when he passed me as I walked up and down the airport, and I smiled back at him.

We joined the slow line onto the plane and found our seats once again.

Soon we were airborne once more. The next leg of the journey was long and tedious over a broad expanse of blue ocean. There was something a little scary about being over deep waters in a metal box (whatever the shape, the plane was still a metal box). Perhaps reading a book would distract me. I pulled out a gardening book *Dick Raymond's Gardening Year*, a gift from Uncle Unny. I enjoyed the easy step-by-step guide to gardening. My mother would love this book too. But my reading was interrupted by another meal and I couldn't remember whether it was breakfast or lunch. But I think this was lunch. Our afternoon movie was the hilarious "*Ghostbusters.*" Once the movie was over, it was time for a bit of rest. However, even as I leaned back into my seat, I wondered if it would soon be time for another meal. I was right when a few minutes later the lights came on and we were served dinner. I suppose all these meals kept the flight crew busy. Otherwise their jobs would be pretty boring—just sitting around waiting for someone to hit the call button for a cup of coffee or an ice-cold Sprite.

It seemed like I'd been on this airplane for a very long time and I was feeling sticky and sweaty. The flight crew, however, always managed to look fresh and calm. I was pretty sure I smelled as bad as I looked. The blue and white cotton tunic I had put on in California was now terribly wrinkled and I felt like I'd lived in my faded comfy Levis for a week. A shower would have been so welcome. Come to think of it Han Soo could have used a good shampoo and scrubbing too. I guess we were all starting to reek a bit like overripe melons.

After the last meal, the lights were dimmed and we were allowed to rest our weary eyes. Another movie started playing on the screen but I was too tired to watch and fell asleep, resting my head on the window.

Much later I woke up with a dry mouth and a trickle of drool running down my chin. Just at that moment a flight attendant was passing by with a tray of hot towels. I used the warm wash cloth on my face, neck and hands. Outside the sky was still inky dark. It must have been nighttime but it was hard for my body to figure out what hour it was. It almost felt like we'd been flying forever with meals served to us every few hours.

There was finally something to see out the window! The sun was rising and the clouds were a beautiful lavender color, touched with pearly gray, beautiful enough for a sari. The lavender slowly changed to a dark pink, and then the world turned golden as the sun peeked out from behind huge poufy clouds. I was glad when we landed in Singapore.

The line to depart moved briskly and I pulled my coat from the overhead bin. Aunt Malathi had insisted I take a trench coat with me.

"The one time I visited Mahagiri I was cold the entire time," she said, as she handed me the tan trench coat. "So you will need this."

I guess when adults were cold, children have to wear coats. My aunt seemed to have forgotten I grew up in Mahagiri and had never needed a coat, but to please her I accepted the gift. Now I really wished I hadn't because I was weighted down with all my carry-on stuff which included a cardboard box filled with samples of Chinese tea and a tea set, complete with tea pot and delicate drinking bowls.

Somehow I managed to carry everything aboard the crowded shuttle bus to the terminal without falling down or dropping something. But once the bus stopped at the terminal and everyone was getting off, I found I couldn't quite pick up everything. I tried shifting the trench coat to my other arm but it was still too difficult to manage all my belongings. I was just about to put on my trench coat, even though it was humid, to free up a hand when someone spoke up, "Here, let me give you a hand."

I looked up into a pair of the darkest brown eyes. I had been prepared to refuse but instead I found myself saying, "Thank you. I guess I could use some help."

He nodded and picked up the box and then looked surprised by its weight.

"What do you have in here? Rocks?"

I smiled. "No. Just a tea set and some tea samples."

"Tea?," he looked down at me as we walked across the hot tarmac. "Planning on drinking a lot of tea, are you?"

"The tea is to share with my family," I said a little huffily. We walked into the cool airport; relieved to be in the air-conditioned building. He turned toward me and I was aware of his good looks. I had to admit to myself he was handsome with even features and dark brown hair that was just a little too long.

"Where are you headed? I can walk you to your gate."

I shook my head and replied, "My connecting flight doesn't leave for several hours. I was going to the lounge."

We walked in silence through the airport.

"This looks like a good place," I said, gesturing to a nearly empty part of the airport. "I can wait here."

I found an empty seat and dropped my backpack and coat. He put the box on the adjacent seat and straightened up.

"Okay, then...goodbye," he said. And they he began to walk away.

"Thanks for your help," I called out.

I was pondering what to do next when he was back at my side.

"Listen, I was thinking. My flight doesn't leave for several hours either. If you want I can watch your bags so that you can use the restroom. They even have shower stalls here."

"There's a place to take a shower here?"

A shower sounded so good just then.

"Yeah, it's pretty basic, but yes there is a place."

"I'd love one," I said.

"Okay, come on," he said, once again picking up the heavy box.

We made our way to the other end of the airport where a sign pointed us to *Lockers for rent. Showers and towel rentals*

We found some seats nearby and put all my stuff down. He seemed to be carrying only a small bag and a garment bag.

Must be nice to travel so lightly.

"I'll go first," he said. "Then you can go and I'll watch your things."

I nodded and sat down. He picked up his duffel bag and disappeared into the showers. I looked around the airport which was a busy place. The shops were open for business and since it was close to lunch, there were quite a lot of people milling around. The tiny cafes and restaurants were crowded.

He came back out looking casual and handsome in clean blue jeans and a black cotton t-shirt. His hair was wet and slicked back.

"Your turn," he announced.

Luckily, I had a change of clothes in my backpack. The shower room was spare but very clean. The attendant was an old lady who presided over a pile of clean white towels. A sign above her head indicated that the cost of the shower and towel was one Singapore dollar. That is when I realized I had no money in local currency. I was about to turn around and leave the room when she stopped me. With hand gestures and a few words of English she indicated that the man outside had paid for my shower and towel rental. I thanked her and entered the shower stall. I turned on the hot water and found a bit of soap wrapped in cellophane and a minuscule bottle of shampoo and conditioner. I used all of it. I had brought a sari with me to change into before seeing my mother. I didn't want her to think I wore only wore jeans and skirts. It was a lavender one that my aunt Malathi had found in a fabric store. The pale purple cloth was sprinkled with tiny gold dots and I had a matching blouse. My hair was too long and thick to dry so I just pinned it away from my face and left it hanging down my back. I again thanked the attendant and handed her an American dollar bill. She accepted it and gave me a toothless grin.

"Pretty girl and nice boy," she said.

I smiled and walked back outside. He was sitting casually in his chair with his long legs sprawled out in front of him. When he saw he me he sat up, dropping the papers he was looking at.

"Wow. You clean up really nice."

I blushed.

"Thanks for paying for the shower."

"I realized you probably don't have Singaporean cash."

"Lucky that you did," I said. "Because I didn't."

"I travel a lot;" he replied "I have change from a lot of places. I have coins from Holland, Tokyo and Germany."

"Wow," I said. "You do travel all over. For business?"

"Yep. For my dad.

"And I just realized I don't know your name," he added.

"Meena, short for Meenaskhi Unnikrishanan," I replied.

He introduced himself. "Raj, Raj Kumar."

We grinned at each other, until he asked, "How about some coffee or food?"

"Something to drink sounds good; I'm still stuffed from all the meals on the plane."

"How about we rent a locker and put our stuff in it?"

Before putting our things away, I pulled out my handbag from my backpack. We made our way through the airport, looking for a café that was not too busy.

"It feels good to stretch my legs," I said.

"It does," he agreed. "I can't wait to get to Bombay and go for a jog."

"I love running too."

We found an open table at a small café and ordered drinks. We sat back and I asked him about his family.

"I have three sisters. Sujata or Suji is married and lives in Delhi. My second sister Pushpa is in college. She wants to go to medical school in the States when she finishes her bachelor's degree. My youngest sister is Saradha, Sara, who is still in high school."

He had just taken a sip of his foamy cappuccino drink and I smiled when I saw his milky moustache.

"What?" he asked.

"You have a cappuccino moustache."

He used his fingers to wipe it away but missed a bit of foam stubbornly clinging to the corner of his mouth.

"Here," I said and leaned over with a napkin.

His fingers gripped my wrist and for a moment time froze as stared at each other. I was aware of his warm fingers on my wrist. If this had been a romantic movie we would have kissed. Someone talking loudly at the next table broke the spell. He turned my wrist over and looked down at the stained napkin.

"Thanks," he said.

I shrugged and he let go of my arm and for an instant I missed the warm pressure of his fingers on my arm.

"I guess I should learn to use a napkin," he said with a slight laugh.

I smiled. "Tell me more about your family." I said, and he started talking. I sat back and listened.

His father, who had started his business with a loan from his brother, had built it into a prosperous enterprise. A self-made man he always liked to keep a keen eye on the whole operation.

Even though his father knew nothing about computers or technology he could see that industry was the future and had invested his money in a small startup company. With the profit, his father had bought an old building near a patch of land that was being used as a dumping ground. He had renovated the building into a hotel and turned the small space behind the hotel into an inviting garden. Eventually the garden became a community garden and even though once in while people tried to steal the produce, the spot had become a safe haven. From this one hotel he had expanded his business and it now included several other hotels, all with attached community gardens and green space. He also had interests in a solar startup and in a company providing wireless service.

I told him all about my mother, the twins, Devi and Muthi. But mostly I talked about Mahagiri.

"I loved living in California but my heart is in Mahagiri," I told him. "There's something about that place, high up in the mountains that touches my spirit. The air is cool and refreshing and some people complain it's always too cold but I find it invigorating. The hills look like they are carpeted in green and on cool winter mornings you can smell the eucalyptus oil in the breeze. Living away for four years has made it clear to me that Mahagiri is the place where I want to be."

Raj was quiet for a moment before saying, "You are lucky to have found such a place. I like Bombay but it doesn't tug at my heart like Mahagiri does for you."

It was enjoyable to just sit back and chat. We must have talked for hours. The day had just slipped by. Night was falling in Singapore and everything was winding down in the airport. I should have been exhausted but I felt energized and wished the day would never end. All around us shop keepers were busy closing up the tiny boutiques, stalls and perfume stores. Steel doors were closed and lights turned off. The airport promenade was not as busy. We left the café and found a small restaurant. Raj ordered us bowls of soup. I was pleasantly surprised at the flavors in the bowl. There were thick rice noodles floating in the sweet-sour broth. Coconut milk, Thai basil and chunks of green papaya added to the taste. The delicate flavor of lemon grass added a subtle aroma.

"This is delicious," I said.

"Don't sound so surprised," he replied. "When you travel a lot you learn how to find good food."

Soon it was time to go pick up my things from the locker because my flight was getting ready to board soon. Raj walked with me to the gate.

"Thanks for the snacks and soup," I said, taking back with my tea set. "The hours just flew by."

"It was fun."

"What are you going to do next?"

"I have to call my dad to see if I return tonight or if I have to attend another meeting."

We stood there for a moment, awkward, shy and a little tongue-tied. Both of us started to say something at the same time.

"You first," I said.

"I was just going to say that I'm glad your aunt made you carry that coat with you because it gave us a chance to meet."

I wanted to say something brilliant and unforgettable but I couldn't find the right words.

"Don't drink all that tea by yourself," he said with a slight smile.

"I don't plan to. My friend Mac will help me?"

"Mac? Who is that?"

"That's my Scottish friend in Mahagiri. Remember, I told you about him?"

"I don't think you mentioned his name though," Raj said.

"Maybe not. But Mac is a good friend and I hope he'll like the different kinds of teas I brought."

"I have a feeling he will love them."

Just then there was an announcement on the loud speakers, calling my flight number.

"I better go," I said reluctantly.

"Bye, Meena. Have a good flight home."

I joined the line of passengers waiting to board. When I reached the agent I handed her my boarding pass and looked back. Raj was still standing at the entryway, watching me. He lifted a hand and I waved back.

CHAPTER 23
RAJ

Raj had watched the young woman struggle with her backpack, jacket and purse. *Come on, someone help her.* But of course this was not America. He had spent some time in New York and knew despite popular opinion most New Yorkers were willing to help. In any case, she wasn't an anonymous person on the street. She was a fellow passenger. She was dressed in an Indian-style kurta top and jeans. Even without the tunic top he could tell she was Indian. There was something about Indian women, the way they held their heads, at once shy and challenging. Or could it be the way Indian women moved? They all seemed to have a distinctive feminine way of walking that other cultures just didn't possess. All his sisters certainly had that gait, even his youngest sister. Being the only guy, besides his father, in a household of women he was very aware of these characteristics.

He had first caught a glimpse of her as she stepped onto the bus and he'd wondered where she was going to find the room for all her belongings, but somehow she did and had stayed upright in the swaying vehicle. And now she was right in front of him. Other passengers stepped past her in the aisle as they hurried on their way. Her things were piled up by her feet. He wasn't sure she would accept his assistance. He watched her long thick braid slip over her shoulder and get in her face. She impatiently flicked the braid back over her shoulder and then looked up at him.

"Thank you. I guess I could use some help."

He followed her into the airport terminal and he couldn't help but admire the way her jeans fit her. He placed the box on a chair in one of the lounges and had started to walk away. But he found he couldn't just leave and so he had gone back. He was glad he did.

CHAPTER 24
MEENA

The plane was full, and I found myself in the middle seat. This part of the trip was short but was made challenging by passengers who were determined to treat the plane as their own home. They spread out their belongings. Families visited each other, talking in loud voices, and ignored the "buckle your seatbelt signs." The crew had a difficult time getting them to sit down, store their luggage and buckle up.

Just as the breakfast service was coming to an end, the plane hit some turbulence. The pilot informed us it was nothing to worry about, just the tail end of a monsoon storm. This bumpy ride meant all those passengers who had gobbled up their Indian veg or non-veg meals were now throwing it all up. The scent of vomit is never a pleasant traveling companion. I was just thankful that my neither of my seatmates were sick.

At one point the plane lost altitude at an alarming rate and even I was shocked out of my complacency and clutched the armrests tightly. The plane's downward dip did dangerous things to my insides and I closed my eyes. The image I saw behind my closed eyelids was the last sight of Raj waving at me from the gates. I guess there was no use thinking about him since there was no chance our paths would cross again. We had no way of contacting one another.

CHAPTER 25
RAJ

As he waited for the phone call from his father to connect, Raj realized with a jolt that he had not asked for Meena's phone number or address. At least he knew she lived in Mahagiri in what was known as the Big House. Did he subconsciously not want to stay in touch with her? He shook his head. No, he wanted to see her again. But she wasn't like those girlfriends of his at UCLA. He couldn't very well ring her up and ask her out for dinner. Anyway in India that was out of the question. There had to be a way. Working for his father these past three years had taught him that every problem had a solution. Sometimes the solution had to be creative. He would find a way to see her again.

CHAPTER 26
MEENA

FAMILIAR SIGHTS

It was late at night, almost dawn, when we landed at Madras International Airport. Although I was anxious to get off the aircraft, I wanted to avoid all the pushing and shoving so I waited until most of the passengers had exited the plane before making my way out. The sun was still low on the eastern horizon, but it was already hot and muggy in Madras. I felt the humidity hug my body like a wet blanket as soon as I stepped off the airplane onto the tarmac. It was just a brief walk to the bus that would take me to the terminal, and even though it was humid, the fresh air felt good after the stuffy airplane.

I waited impatiently with other passengers for our bags to be unloaded from the plane. Finally, the lights above a carousel began to flash and suitcases start to flow out. I spotted my two black suitcases with their pink and yellow ribbons and stepped forward to the carousel to retrieve them.

I lugged the bags onto a cart and headed to the line for immigration. The family in front of me was asked to open every piece of luggage. Even though their baby was squirming and their toddler was whimpering, the officers took their time going through diapers and jars of baby food.

When it was my turn the officer looked at me with a bored expression.

"Anything to declare?" he asked with a sleepy look.

Nothing except your attitude.

"No," I said firmly.

But something about my voice caught his attention and he sat up, "Let's see, shall we?"

I opened the largest of my suitcases. There was no point in fighting Indian bureaucracy. Among the clothes I had tucked in seed packets and plastic net bags of purple, yellow and red potatoes.

The officer used his night stick to poke around. He pulled out a T-shirt and held it high. Seeing nothing, he dropped it back in the suitcase. He then used his hands to rummage around. He gave me a triumphant look as he pulled out a pink plastic box containing my sanitary napkins. He glared at me as he fumbled with the catch. When he finally had it open, he dumped the contents on top of my open suitcase. He was not expecting to see the wrapped napkins. A fellow officer stopped stamping passports to watch him and snickered out loud. The immigration officer blushed, his features turning an ugly dark color.

"Off with you," he said, stamping my passport. "Take all this rubbish and get out of the way. Quickly now."

I stuffed all my clothes back in, angered by the intrusion into my privacy.

"Welcome to India," I mumbled to myself.

The officer must have heard my comment because he glared at me again. I stared back at him with a defiant look and then I made my way from the international terminal to the national one. After a short wait I was soon boarding a plane to Pellaur. This plane was tiny and I could feel the engine reverberating beneath my feet, almost as if it wanted to escape from the plane. I hoped it flew better than it sounded.

The hour-long trip was actually not bad. The crew served

us coffee, proper south Indian coffee. Before I knew it we were landing at the tiny Pellaur Airport. I could feel my heart thumping with excitement at the thought of seeing my mother again. I had missed her so much after being away for four years. My uncle had offered to send me back but I knew that the financial burden would be too much for him and my mother. So I had stayed away, going to summer school and working at the college farm. Now I was finally going to see my family.

Things were more informal at Pellaur. When I stepped off the plane, I had to walk only a few paces to enter the airport. My family was waiting in the lobby. I couldn't believe how tall the twins were. Appu looked like he had grown a foot taller. Muthi and my mother were also there, wearing huge welcoming grins. Everyone was talking at once and there was a lot of hugging and laughing. We made our way to the baggage claim area as one joyous group. I hugged the twins, glad to see them again.

"You two are so big now," I said.

Appu grinned at me. "And you've shrunk, big sister."

He was taller than me and was still the reserved little boy I remembered. Thangam was her usual self, talkative and affectionate. My mother looked older and there were many white strands in her hair but she looked happy and relaxed. Muthi looked ageless.

"Muthi, you look the same," I said to her as we made our way to the car. "You haven't aged one day."

"Ahh.. *kutty*. I have many aches and pains. I wish your Ayah were here with her remedies."

Ayah was my old nanny who had a knack for home remedies and was known for her healing potions and herbs.

Jaibal, our driver, was waiting by the car, a huge grin on his face.

"You are no longer a kutty," he said to me.

"I haven't been for a long time, Jaibal."

"But she will be always be *my kutty*," my mother said, coming up and putting her arm around my waist. "Are you hungry, Meena? We can stop and get something to eat. Devi is planning a feast for this evening."

"Then I'll wait," I said. "I'm ready to go home."

It was snug in the car with all the passengers and bags, but we all managed to squeeze in and soon we were on our way. There were snacks— banana chips, early plums from our garden and a handful of tiny red guavas. I shared stories about California and my uncle and aunt as we drove

"How is Chitra?" my mother asked.

"She's going to law school soon," I said. "She's always busy."

I told them about my visit to New York to see Kumari.

"Will she come back to Mahagiri?" Thangam asked.

I shrugged my shoulders, "She said she would be coming for a visit but I think she likes New York."

"I'm glad you are back," Appu said with quiet smile.

"Me too," I replied. "I can't wait to show you all the stuff I brought home."

CHAPTER 27
MEENA

HOME AGAIN

It was late afternoon when we arrived home and I was glad to get out of the car. I stretched and took a deep breath of Mahagiri air which was tinged with the scent of late spring flowers from my mother's garden. The twins and Jaibal carried my bags into the house and I walked around to the back. My mother and Muthi followed me. The garden was bathed in light. I could see the bamboo poles standing upright, ready for the tomato vines and green bean plants. Everything was blooming and flourishing. Mahagiri summer was just around the corner.

"All this looks wonderful, Amma. Even better than I remembered."

"I have a lot of help these days," my mother said. "From your letters it sounds like you are quite the farmer woman now?"

I laughed, "Yes, Amma, I did change my major from Biology to Agricultural Science. I even have an idea that I want to run by Mac. How is he, by the way?"

"He's old but still going strong. I haven't seen him in a few weeks but Miss Mala comes to visit Muthi and brings all the news."

After my tour of the garden, I visited Devi in the kitchen.

"Kutty, it seems like yesterday that you were in here saying goodbye," she said.

"I know, Devi. I can't believe how much time has gone by and how some things never change, like this kitchen."

"A kitchen is just stones and brick," Devi said. "The spirit of the kitchen is what you carry with you wherever you go."

That evening we gathered in the dining room for a joyous feast. Bhojan was there with Raman and Kashi. Kashi's son was now a five-year-old and they had a beautiful baby girl as well.

"Meena, I so wanted to name her after you but my father said it would be better to name her after your mother. This is Sudhadevi."

"She's beautiful, Kashi. The name suits her. Two Meenas might be too much."

We giggled together and it really seemed as if I had never left.

Devi had outdone herself with mounds of steaming hot Basmati rice, fresh ghee, tangy Aviyal Stew, creamy Potato/ Ginger Stew, garlic broth, green beans and cauliflower. But the real surprise was dessert which consisted of thin buttery pancakes filled with last year's pear jam.

"What is this?" I asked Devi, taking a bite.

"You aren't the only one cooking Western food," she said. "Muthi learned how to make them from Mala. They are Scottish pancakes with Little Mother's pear jam."

After the meal we gathered in the living room and I opened my suitcases and pulled out the gifts. The different colored potatoes and seed packets were a big hit with Bhojan, Raman and my mother. They were already making plans on how to use them in the next planting. I had brought back puzzles, books, some small toys and pieces of cloth for the ladies.

"This will make a nice sari blouse," Kashi said admiring a piece of orange-yellow cloth.

I also had chocolates, candies and gum. The twins showed Kashi's son Mohan how to chew gum and blow bubbles.

My mother had installed a telephone and I slipped out of the room to place a call to Mac. His booming voice filled the ear-piece.

"Meena! You are back. It is good to hear your voice. After you get settled in, come by for a chat."

I promised and went to attend our evening Pooja ceremony. As the familiar scents and sounds enveloped me I closed my eyes, thankful to have returned home.

CHAPTER 28
RAJ

Raj woke up a little bleary eyed. He had not slept well, tossing and turning and dreaming of girls in purple saris. Jeez, when had he become such a sap? Mooning over a girl he had met and spent just a few hours with? He must really be losing it.

A hot shower followed by several cups of strong coffee made him feel like he could cope with the day's business. Watching the planes take off as he waited for his flight reminded him of Meena. He shook his head, impatient with himself. It was only when he was seated in the business section of the airplane that he had the privacy and time to really give in to his thoughts of her. All day she had been in the back of his mind; a tiny warm feeling. He shifted again. It was going to be a long flight.

He refused the food and chose to sleep and even though it took some time, he eventually dozed off. He woke up when the cabin lights came on and accepted some cranberry juice and a cup of coffee. The croissant and jam were perfect for now but he would need something more substantial when he got off the plane.

When the plane finally taxied into the terminal at New Delhi, he was one of the first to get off. He was impatient to take the connecting flight to Bombay. The New Delhi terminal was busy as always and he found the railway café to be filled with many young families. He ordered a Western breakfast even though he knew it would be nothing like what he was used to in California. He looked around at the couples and families, was everyone married these days?

The connecting flight to Bombay was uneventful and soon he was landing in Bombay's Chatrapati Shivaji International Airport. It was warm and muggy, with a hint of rain on the horizon. The southwest monsoon season was in full swing with bands of heavy rain followed by muggy weather. It was fortunate that his flight had landed just as the rains had abated because during the monsoons cancellations and delays were the norm.

As expected, he went through immigration without much delay or hassle. Business travelers were less scrutinized. His bags had made it through and he picked up his suitcase and headed outside.

He had just exited the baggage claim area when he saw the smiling face of his father. The old man actually had come to meet him!

"Dad." Raj reached out to hug his father with one arm. "You didn't have to come. I could have taken a taxi."

"Ah, it's good to see you son and besides your mother is going crazy over the Deepavali celebrations. She wants to invite everyone so I thought it best to give her some space."

Raj's father gave him an appraising look. "I trust everything went well?"

"Yes, the meetings were great," he replied. "I've written up reports on all of them and you can read them as soon as we get home."

"Good, good." His father nodded as he stroked his moustache. "It is just as we thought?"

"Yes, Dad," Raj said. "There were no surprises."

The driver and car were parked in the loading zone and Dinesh, their family chauffeur, leapt out of the car, and opened the trunk.

"Dinesh, good to see you," Raj greeted him.

"Good to have you back, Raj sir."

"I've only been gone a three months, Dinesh."

"Yes, but a lot has been happening," his father said.

Dinesh was just a few years older than him and had been a member of his boyhood cricket team. They smiled at each other, comfortable as only old friends can be.

His father climbed in the back with Raj.

"Deepavali is not for months," Raj said. "Why is Ma already planning?"

His father shook his head, "You know how she is. She wants this one to be special because you are home now and your sister has finally finished her pre-med requirements."

"So Pushpa is home?"

"Not yet. She is applying to medical schools including a couple in the US and so she will join us later, probably after the monsoon season."

"So Ma is out of control?"

"Celebrations are her thing and she is definitely on the warpath. And she's also been muttering about weddings. So be prepared."

Raj looked out the window and was silent for a moment. The lights of the main city faded as they turned away from the busy part of town. Their house was on a hillside overlooking the ocean and already he could see the evening lights twinkling to his left. It looked like it would be a clear night until the clouds burst and the world turned wet. Warm, fat raindrops fell fast and furious. The monsoon season was here. Great, he sighed to himself. Welcome to Bombay, the city that was never really dry during the rainy season.

He turned back to his father, "As long as it's not my wedding she's planning," he joked.

His father's almost somber expression was comical.

"What? You mean it is?"

"I'm not saying that, son, but she's been meeting with various people."

"People? What kind of people?"

"You know, astrologers and such."

"But Dad, we aren't living in olden times. I thought we had an understanding."

His father shook his head and smoothed his gray moustache, a sign he was troubled. His expression was still solemn.

"Son, all understanding goes out the window when your mother makes up her mind. She thinks that at 26 you are old enough to marry and give her grandchildren."

Grandchildren? Was his mother really planning out his future? Meena's smile crossed his mind for a moment and he shook his head to get rid of the image.

"I'm going to have to talk to her," he muttered to himself. "I'm just not ready to settle down."

"Well, let's just change the subject, then. Tell me more about the business meetings."

The rest of the ride they talked business and the fact Raj had met with certain foreign investors looking to invest in India. Wouldn't Mahagiri be the perfect location? He would have to share the idea with his dad. Perhaps he could convince his dad he needed to visit Mahagiri to scope out the place. But first he would have to talk his mother out of arranging his marriage. She was stubborn and he wasn't looking forward to speaking with her.

The car stopped on front of the spacious curved driveway and Dinesh jumped out to open car doors before Raj could unfold himself from the back seat.

Raj paused and looked at the driver, "Thanks, Dinesh. Is there a cricket game on tomorrow?"

"On Mondays, Wednesdays and Fridays at the Grounds," Dinesh said.

The Grounds was probably the last patch of undeveloped land in Bombay and was a popular place for pick-up cricket games.

"Perhaps I'll join you tomorrow or Friday," he said to Dinesh, who smiled back at him

He followed his father up the stairs and into the wide hallway. The lights were all blazing and he called out, "Ma, we are here."

"You have finally come, my son," my mother said with a meaningful look.

Raj smiled at his mother's dramatic words and put down the suitcase to hug her. She clasped him in her arms and then pushed him away to look at him.

"Hmm, you look healthy," she said.

"And you look as beautiful as ever," he replied with a laugh.

His mother *was* beautiful, tall, slim and fashionably dressed in the latest designer sari and blouse. Her white hair was cut in an elegant bob and she carried herself with a quiet sophistication.

"Bapu, you are home safe too," she said to my father, touching his shoulder with affection.

Are you hungry?" she asked. "Kavitha has gone to bed but she left you some poori masala. Shall I heat it up?"

"Thanks Ma. I'm a little hungry but first I need to go upstairs and change. These clothes have been on too many public seats."

Raj started up the stairs, pausing at the mid-way landing and glancing down. He could see his parents talking in low voices, heads bent close together. For a moment he envied their closeness. His sister's door was shut, and he walked quietly down the hallway to his own room. He turned on the light; everything was as he had left it. He took a quick shower before changing into a pair of comfortable Indian-style cotton pants and a loose cotton top.

His mother had a plate of food ready for him on the dining room table when he came back downstairs.

"Come sit down and tell me your adventures. You did have some didn't you?"

He went to the side board and poured himself a soda water, dropping a couple of ice cubes.

"Ma, I was in meetings all the time. I didn't even get to eat at any good restaurants."

"We'll have to change all that," his mother said. "We have been invited to a very posh party tomorrow night and you have to come."

Raj sighed.

"I think I need to check in at the office, right, Dad?"

His father held up his hands in a gesture of surrender. "Hey, don't look at me for an excuse. If I have to go to this party, then so do you."

"All right," Raj agreed reluctantly. "I'll go."

CHAPTER 29
MEENA

The next morning, I forced myself to stay in bed until I heard sounds coming from the kitchen. I wanted to combat the lingering effects of jet lag and be back on Mahagiri time. When I could no longer bear it, I got up. It was comforting to sit in the busy kitchen and sip hot coffee. Devi was fussing over breakfast, determined to make the delicate rice dumplings I enjoyed so much. The air was fragrant with the sourdough smell of steaming rice dumplings and the strong aroma of coffee. The coffee was tasty with an unusual flavor.

"What's in the coffee?" I asked.

Devi smiled. "We all love cardamom in our tea and I thought how about putting some in the coffee. Do you like it?"

"I do," I said, taking another sip. "It's very different and gives the bitter coffee a nice sweet flavor."

"What happened to Radha?" I asked Devi.

Devi paused for a moment and shook her head.

"Radha, you know, left the planation and came here. Murthy and Paru Amma didn't want her to leave Chandur but Radha was determined and your mother agreed to have her come here for a visit. Your mother encouraged her to attend the typing school in Upper Mahagiri. Every morning she would get up and go to her typing and shorthand class and in the afternoon she helped me in the kitchen. She was a very nice and smart girl. She had been here about six months when we had a visitor one afternoon.

"It was a man dressed in military uniform which scared Muthi. The man was from the barracks on St. Anthony Road. Remember that place?"

I nodded. The Indian Army housed their officers in a group of buildings that stood at the edge of the local golf course. On my trips to Upper Mahagiri I had seen soldiers running along the roadside, carrying heavy backpacks and wearing sturdy boots.

"Well, the man," Devi continued, "was an officer from the barracks named Anish. Apparently Anish had seen Radha at the bus top and wanted to talk to her. She had refused and now he had come to see your mother to ask for her hand in marriage.

"We were all surprised," Devi said seeing my expression. "But your mother met with the man's superior and found out that he was an orphan who had joined the army and slowly worked his way to officer rank. He seemed like a nice young man.

"After nearly a month of visits and conversations, they were married here."

"At our house?" I asked.

"Yes in sitting room, right next to Pooja room. We decorated the sitting area with garlands and vases of fresh flowers. A priest came and performed the ceremony. The twins were very excited. Then we had a party in the front yard. Bhojan hung lights in all the trees and I prepared a proper Kerala feast with everything including brown sugar payasam. Anish had some friends come over and we played music. It was a lovely wedding."

"What did Paru Amma think of all this?"

"Oh, she was skeptical and unhappy at first. For some reason they thought she and Anand might get together. But Radha wasn't interested in him at all."

I added, "Actually there was a girl at the plantation who was interested in Anand."

I remembered how Anand and Rani had exchanged glances when I was at the planation four years ago. I had thought a romance might be brewing between them.

"So I heard. He's married to Rani now," Devi said. "Anyway, Radha lives in the barracks now and has a one year old boy."

"I'm glad she is happy," I said. "Her mother was so worried about her and she really didn't want to live in Chandur for the rest of her life. As an Army wife she will get to travel and experience a different kind of life."

"Meena," Devi said in a hesitant voice. She had a troubled look on her face. "I don't know if I should tell you this or not."

It was not like Devi to be hesitant about voicing her opinion. She had always said out loud what she thought. That's why my mother valued her opinion so much.

"What is it, Devi?"

She shook her head and walked over to the table. She sat down on a stool next to me.

"Meena, your mother may be in trouble."

"What are you saying, Devi?"

"You know the land just below the cowshed?"

Devi was referring to the open space, a beautiful meadow just below the hillside on one side of our house. My mother bought this piece of land from our neighbor, an older man who lived in the village behind us.

"Yes," Devi nodded. "Well, there seems to be some question about who owns that meadow."

"But mother bought it from Shivalingam a long time ago," I said.

"I know that, kutty, but now a new owner has the property and he's coming to meet your mother to talk about it."

"Why didn't mother mention this?"

"She didn't want to spoil your homecoming."

"Do you know when the meeting is going to happen?"

"They are coming for tea today."

I wanted to talk to my mother but she was busy in the garden and so I decided to go for a run to clear my mind. I was bursting with energy and the need to do something.

I changed into sweats and pulled my running shoes out from the suitcase. To warm up I walked through our fruit orchard. The trees were filled with green peaches. They wouldn't be ripe for a few more weeks, but the mulberries were plump and reminded me of big fat purple worms but that didn't stop me from popping one in my mouth. The fruit was juicy and sweet.

I walked to the edge of the orchard until I came to a well-worn dirt path. I started to run, following the path through bright green tea bushes and out of the tea plantation to a small side road, which was lined giant eucalyptus trees. It was a perfect day for a jog. The air was fragrant with the leafy scent of fallen eucalyptus leaves and acorns. I picked up my pace as I wound around the narrow road and started up the hill. This path led me to fields just below my house. I stopped running when I reached the edge of our front yard. I walked around to the back where I found my mother in the garden with Bhojan and Raman.

"What have you been doing, kutty?" Bhojan asked.

I knew better than to ask him not to call me kutty.

"I went for a run. I ran through the orchard and down Eucalyptus Lane,"

"What are you running from?" he said.

I tried to explain but my mother stepped in, "Bhojan, it is what people do when they are not out working like you. Since they are inside most of the time, they feel all cramped up and they need to stretch their legs."

Bhojan nodded, "So this is something you learned in America?"

I had to laugh. "Yes. And it is supposed to make you healthy."

"Alright," he said good-naturedly. "But I think I'm healthy enough digging potatoes and milking cows."

I couldn't argue with that.

"Amma, I need to talk to you," I pulled her aside.

Seeing my serious expression, my mother nodded.

"Devi told you, didn't she?" she asked.

"Yes, Amma. But don't blame her," I said. "Tell me what's going on."

"I really don't know," she said with a heavy sigh. "I bought the land from Shivalingam and now I hear a corporation has bought the adjoining property and wants to meet with me. They sent me a letter requesting a meeting about the meadow, saying there is some dispute about who owns the land."

She added, "They are coming today to discuss this with me. Bhojan is going to stay for the meeting."

I didn't say anything but I was not about to miss the meeting. I had wanted to talk to my mother about growing Chinese tea but decided this was not the time to spring a new idea on her. She looked too worried and stressed.

CHAPTER 30
MEENA

THE MEETING

Devi had made lemon rice for lunch but the tart grains stuck to my throat and I had a hard time swallowing. The creamy potato and ginger stew with sweet coconut milk helped soothe my nervous stomach. After leaving instructions with Muthi that the twins were not to disturb us when they came back from school, my mother and I waited in the living room for our guest.

"Little mother," Bhojan entered the room. "They are here."

Two gentlemen followed him into the room. Both were tall, with curly hair and handsome features. There were definitely father and son and both of them were impeccably dressed in tailored suits.

"Little Mother," the older man spoke in a clipped British accent. "I hope you don't mind me calling you by that name, but I hear that is what everyone calls you.

My mother smiled," You have done your homework ,Mr. Menon."

"Ah, please call me Suresh. I see you have done your research too."

He folded his palms together in a traditional greeting. My mother returned the greeting and nodded.

"This is my daughter, Meena, and my manager, Bhojan. Please sit down."

"And this is my son, Devrat."

Devrat greeted us with folded palms. "Please call me Dev; you have a beautiful place here."

The rose garden was in full bloom in our side yard and the fragrance of the blooms drifted in through the open window.

"Thank you, Dev," my mother said.

Just then Muthi entered with a tray of tea and snacks. After everyone had received a cup of hot tea and a plate of salted cashews and plantain chips, my mother cleared her throat.

"Please," Suresh interrupted her. "Can I speak?"

He didn't wait for a reply, but put down his tea cup on the table and leaned forward.

"I'm part of a corporation that has bought land just over the hill from your property. Eventually, we hope to develop that parcel of land into a resort and a housing complex. As you know the meadow is the piece of land that divides our properties."

"Yes," my mother said. "I bought that meadow several years ago from the landowner Shivalingam. I have the deeds right here."

"I understand that you bought the property in good faith, Little Mother," Suresh said. "But we looked at the title when we bought the adjoining acreage and discovered something."

Suresh sat back and picked up his tea cup. He took a sip and stared at us. Both men were looking at us with greedy eyes. Perhaps that was my imagination.

"What did you find?" my mother's voice was calm, but I knew she was not feeling very calm.

"The property belonged to his brother Ramalingam and Shivalingam had no right to sell it. We just bought it from Ramalingam."

My mother said nothing.

Bhojan snorted from his chair. He hated sitting in my mother's presence and was perched on the edge.

156

"That is not true. Everyone in the village knows that Ramalingam lost the property in a game of cards to his brother."

Suresh looked at Bhojan with a patronizing expression. "Maybe he did but the brothers never changed the name on the title."

That meadow had special meaning for our family. My mother had bought the property several years ago so that a group of wandering gypsies would have a place to stay when they visited Mahagiri. Now that land would be gone forever. I knew my gypsy friend Priya would probably never come back but the land would have been a memory to her and her family. I swallowed a lump of sadness in my throat. I looked up and was startled to see Suresh looking at me. I felt my face grow hot and red under his scrutiny.

Both men stood up. We did the same.

"Little mother," Suresh said. "We'd like to be good neighbors and hope we can be friends."

He turned to his son, "Dev, please go on outside, I have one more thing to discuss with Little Mother in private."

Dev and Bhojan started toward the door. Suresh turned to me, "Please Meena, I need a word with your mother, please excuse us."

I reluctantly followed the men, wondering what Suresh wanted to say to my mother.

I found Dev waiting for me on the porch steps.

"Ah, Meena," he said. "Do I detect an American accent?"

I laughed, "Hardly. My cousin Chitra's accent is much stronger. You sound so British."

"That's because most of my schooling was in England. My mom is actually English."

"So you are planning on moving to Mahagiri?"

"Are you joking? No. I'm just here with my dad. What about you?"

"This is my home. I love it here."

"No way, are you serious? This is a place time forgot. Last night we were awakened by the local tribe. They sounded like they were partying and killing some animal."

I stiffened. He sounded so arrogant. Bhojan had an angry look on his face.

"That wasn't a party. It was a funeral and the screaming you heard were the women mourners weeping."

"Whatever," Dev shrugged his shoulders. "I have no interest in them or this place."

I was about to tell him off when my mother and Suresh came down the porch steps.

"Bye Meena, good to meet you," Suresh said as they left. Dev waved and Bhojan closed the gate behind the men.

"Amma," I turned to my mother.

"Not now, Meena," my mother rubbed her forehead. "I have to go lie down for a while."

She left without another word.

"Bhojan, what do you think happened?" I asked our manager.

He shook his head.

"Those men are not good men," he said. "I'm glad we will have nothing more to do with them."

It turned out Bhojan was wrong.

CHAPTER 31
MEENA

BAD NEWS

My mother did not come out her room for the rest of the day. Devi took her a tray of soothing garlic broth and yogurt rice. She came back with a grim face.

"Your mother just wants to be left alone."

Somehow we got the twins in bed and closed down the kitchen for the night. I spent a restless night, dreaming I was being chased by unknown monsters. I woke up sweating and hot, even though the room was cool.

The next morning, my mother was nowhere to be seen. I helped with the milking and getting the twins ready for school. It was nearly mid-morning when Devi, Muthi and I gathered in the kitchen. I had barely touched my breakfast and was sipping on my third cup of coffee and was feeling a bit jittery. I would have to go for a run soon to get rid of all this excessive energy. My mother walked in the kitchen. She looked awful.

"Amma," I rushed toward her.

"Meenakutty," she said, hugging me. "We have to talk."

Devi handed her a cup of hot coffee and Muthi led her to a mat. She sat down and leaned against the wall. I sat beside her, loving the feel of her warm body next to mine.

"What's going on, Amma?"

My mother took a sip of her drink and then set it down beside her. She shook her head and sighed deeply.

"When you were gone, we had quite a few setbacks. One year there was no rain and the next year there was too much. All that affected our crops. Even our cows didn't produce milk. We were in dire straits."

"I thought Achan's estate money would have helped," I said.

"It did, but we used most of it for your plane tickets and other college expenses."

I was quiet. I remembered spending my monthly pocket money on what now seemed like frivolous things. I was buying lipstick and mascara while my mother was pinching her paisas.

"I'm sorry, Amma."

She hugged me closer.

"It wasn't your fault, Meena. I also made some bad investments. Mac and I thought it would be a good idea to plant grape vines on his southern slopes."

I was surprised to hear that Mac would ask my mother to be part of any bad or hasty investment, but my mother was still talking.

"In any case, I had to use our house as collateral to borrow from the bank. I have been making monthly payments but now…"

All three of us tensed as she paused.

Muthi spoke first, "I knew those men were bad news. Even Bhojan was saying…."

My mother shook her head, "Yes, it is bad news. The bank has sold my loan to Suresh's company. It was part of some big deal, I don't know all the details, but Suresh says he can call in the loan and if I don't pay the full amount of the loan, I could lose the property and even the house."

Devi and I gasped out loud and Muthi started lamenting in a loud voice.

"Surely, Mac or someone can help us, can't they, Amma?"

"I don't think Mac will have the amount we need, Meena."

We were all silent for a long moment.

"Amma, what are we going to do? We have to find a way," I said, my voice breaking with emotion.

My mother shook her head, her expression full of sorrow and regret.

"But Suresh did give me an option."

We looked at her. "What option?" Devi asked.

My mother looked down at her hands and I couldn't help noticing how tired and haggard she looked. She had aged overnight.

"What did he say, Amma?" I asked, a little impatiently. Why wasn't she happy that there was an option? How bad could it be?

"Meena," she said looking at me with a bleak expression on her face. "Suresh says he will forget about the loan if you agree to marry Dev."

Of all the things I expected, this was not what I was anticipating.

"What?" I shouted. "Marry Dev? You can't be serious, Amma."

"I know this sounds awful but…"

I didn't let my mother finish, "No! You have no idea what kind of man he is. I talked to him while you were meeting with his father and he's arrogant and vain and hates Mahagiri."

I stood up, my fists clenched. I was determined not to burst into tears.

"I know this is not the ideal solution but if we don't discuss this option we could lose everything. We just need to talk about it."

"Amma, you don't know what you are asking."

I couldn't stand it anymore and ran out of the room. I heard my mother calling my name but I didn't turn around.

CHAPTER 32
MEENA

MAC'S ADVICE

I ran through the back door and down to the orchard. My flip-flops were getting in the way and I tossed them aside as I ran. I ignored the sharp stones and twigs on my bare feet. Finally, out of breath I came to a stop at the edge of our back garden. Chest heaving and out of breath I sat down on the small stone bench shaded by a scraggy pear tree. What was my mother thinking? I didn't know how long I had been sitting in the dappled shade until I heard my name.

"Meenakutty?"

I looked up and saw, Muthi standing in front of me with a sad expression in her eyes. She was also carrying my running shoes. I didn't say anything for a long moment and then burst into tears. Muthi sat next to me and put her arm around my shoulder. Finally, I stopped crying.

"Why is she doing this?" I asked, hiccuping a bit.

"Oh, kutty, your mother is trying to do her best. This news about the loan as come has a great shock and I think she doesn't know what else to do."

"What am I to do, Muthi? I love this house but marrying someone just to save it seems so wrong. I'm not sure I can do that but if I don't and we lose our home…"

"Listen to me, Meena. You are too young to carry this burden, my little one. Come, dry your tears and put on your shoes. I have an idea."

I used Muthi's handkerchief to wipe my face and blow my nose. I probably looked a sight with swollen eyelids and red eyes. I put on the shoes and socks and sat up.

"Good," Muthi said. "Now, lets you and I go for a walk."

"Where to?"

"Let's go talk to Mac. He seems to have good advice when you need it and has been a good friend to you."

"I've been meaning to go see him. But I look terrible."

Muthi brushed aside my protest with her hand and soon we were on way. As we started up the hill, I was alarmed at Muthi's labored breathing.

"Muthi, why don't you go back and let Amma know where I'm going and that I might stay the night."

"Are you sure?"

"Yes, I'm sure, Muthi. Please go back."

"I will call Mac and let him know you are on your way." I'm too old to climb that hill," she said, rubbing her knees.

Her remark was a sharp reminder that everyone had aged in the four years I had been away. I wasn't the only one who had grown and changed.

Half way through my hike up the hill, I stopped at the familiar rock to gaze at the view. It was truly breathtaking. The entire valley lay below me like an emerald paradise bathed in the glow of the sun. In the distance I could see the cluster of white-washed houses—one of them would be Raman and Kashi's home. I stared up the gentle slope and soon came into view of the large welcoming bungalow and the spacious gardens. The last time I had come here to visit, Mac had been outside to welcome me. I stopped and looked around but no one was in sight. I wandered up to the porch and knocked on the sturdy wooden doors.

"Coming, coming," a voice called and then Mala was opening the door. "Kutty, you are back and looking so beautiful."

"Thank you, Miss Mala. How are you? Devi made your pancake recipe last night and they were delicious."

"I had to adjust it a bit to make it appealing for us, but it is a tasty Scottish recipe," Mala said. "Come in. The master is waiting for you in the library. He has been like a child, waiting by the front door for you."

"How is he?"

"A little older and slower, but aren't we all? Except you! Here you are all grown-up. I hope your mother is arranging your marriage soon."

I had to stop myself from crying, "Yes, I'm sure she will be."

The older woman looked taken aback at my harsh tone of voice but didn't say anything more. I followed her down a dark hallway and she opened the door to the library, "Miss Meena is here. Shall I bring tea?"

I turned to her, "Not yet, Mala. I need to talk to Mac first." She nodded and left.

I entered the familiar library and as expected there was a roaring fire in the fireplace. Between the golden lamps and the fireplace the room was warm and glowing. Mac was seated in his leather chair by the fire. He got up a little slowly as I entered the room. It was so good to see his familiar face; I went up to him and hugged him tight. As I breathed in the unique Mac aroma of wood smoke, tobacco and wool, I began to cry.

"Meena, what's wrong?"

I couldn't answer because I was sobbing into his chest. Mac said nothing and held me tightly. Finally, I stopped and looked up into his bright blue eyes.

"I'm sorry, Mac," I said stepping me away from him. I've ruined your lovely jacket."

"Never mind about my jacket, are you alright, Meena?"

I nodded and wiped my eyes. Mac handed me his handkerchief and I blew my nose.

"Come sit by the fire," he led me to a large chair. I sank into it and sighed.

I looked across at Mac and felt tears rising again. I wiped them away with the kerchief.

"It's not your mother, is it? Is she ill?"

"Oh, Mac, Amma is fine. I'm sorry I'm such a mess but things are..."

"Go on, you can tell me, Meena. Talk to me."

"Did you know my mother had borrowed money, Mac?"

Mac sat back in his chair. He spoke slowly, "No. Everyone was having a hard time a couple of years ago but I thought your mother bounced back. I'm guessing she didn't?"

"Yesterday we had a couple of visitors who came to tell us a corporation had bought the meadow below our house."

"The one belonging to Shivalingam?"

"Yes, turns out Shivalingam didn't really own the land. His brother Ramalingam still owned the land and he sold it to the corporation."

"Wait, how is that possible? Didn't your mother buy the land from Shivalingam before he died?"

I sighed, "It is all a mess, Mac. My mother thought she was buying the land but she really wasn't. We just found out the title we have is not legal. A couple of corporation guys came to meet my mother yesterday and one of them, a man named Suresh, met with my mother alone."

"I don't understand."

"That makes two," I replied. "Apparently, my mother also took a loan to tide her over when things were bad a couple of years ago and used the house as collateral. Now..."

I couldn't bear to say the words out loud.

"Now, someone is calling the loan?" Mac guessed.

I nodded again. "Yes, turns out Suresh's company bought the bank that now owns the loan. He says...."

I faltered, trying to get the words out.

"He told my mother he wouldn't call in the loan if she agreed to a marriage between me and his son."

"What," Mac stood up and dropped the pipe he was filling. "That is outrageous. This isn't some medieval village. This is illegal. It's blackmail."

His face was getting redder by the minute and for a moment I was worried he was going to choke on his anger and outrage. But he drew a deep breath and turned to me.

"Listen, Meena. I don't know anything about this Suresh fellow but what he is trying to do is immoral and I'm guessing illegal. This isn't going to happen."

"Are you sure, Mac?" my voice was filled with hope.

"Yes, my lass. I'll fight it with everything. Besides, your mother is Little Mother of Mahagiri. Do you think her friends and neighbors will allow her to be bullied? Chin up, my dear. We'll sort it all out. Trust me."

I did trust Mac and so I took a deep breath and finally started to feel a bit more hopeful. Maybe things weren't as bad as I imagined.

Mac saw me sitting up taller and smiled. "That's it. Now we need some strong tea and a ginger scones and you are going to tell me all about America. I'm going to tell Mala to bring us tea and I'm going to telephone your mother and let her know you are spending the night. And I don't want to hear another word about loans, is that understood, Meena?"

I sniffed and brushed the last tears off my face and finally smiled at my friend.

Mac returned a few minutes later and sat down in his chair and looked at me. In the light of the fire, I could see that his hair was whiter and there were more wrinkles on his face.

"My, you are a sight for these eyes. I have missed you, Meena."

I felt happy tears flowing down my face. "I've missed you too, Mac. And you don't look a year older to me."

"Ah, you are a pretty good liar, Meena, but you are the one who is older and more beautiful. You are all grown up."

"Oh, Mac," I said, "I had such a good time in California. During the last two years I've learned so much about tea. I had thought you drank it only with milk and sugar or with lemon like the British but I discovered a whole new world of tea. The Chinese tea ceremony is so calming and peaceful. You would love it."

He laughed at my enthusiasm. "I'm sure I'm going to hear all about it."

Just then Mala came in with a teapot on a tray. She poured us cups of strong tea and handed me a plate of her famous ginger scone.

"Anything else?" she asked looking at Mac and then me. I shook my head and she left the room.

"Mac, I was going to bring my tea set and make you Chinese tea."

"You can tell me about it instead and we can play tea party another day."

I laughed, remembering how much I loved Mac's sense of humor and kindness.

"While I was in California my aunt took me to a shop that served Chinese tea and I liked it so much that I joined the university's International Cultural Center so I could learn more about this ancient tradition."

I took a sip of hot tea, "Interestingly enough the art of drinking tea is known as *chayi* a word that is similar to our chai. There are many versions of the tea ceremony but I thought the one using the small Yixing tea pot would be easiest for us in Mahagiri."

I tried to remember everything I had learned in the few classes and workshops I had attended. I told him all about how to conduct the ceremony to ward off bad *qi* or energy.

Mac leaned forward to take another scone, "So this is all done in a tea shop?"

"Yes. But not an ordinary tea shop. It has to be a special place that is filled with tranquility and peace. Perhaps we can find someplace with a fountain and plenty of greenery because a tea ceremony is calming as well as invigorating."

"Along with tea, we should serve special snacks, dumplings made with soft dough as well as ones wrapped in wonton skins," I said.

I then told him about the Chinese wedding tea ceremony, an elaborate tradition designed to bind and unite families.

I then shared what I had learned about tea.

"Tea is considered one of the seven daily necessities in Chinese life."

"What are the others?" Mac asked.

I used my fingers to list them," Firewood, rice, salt, oil, soy sauce and vinegar."

"Well, if you add chili peppers and coconuts to that list for south Indians," Mac said.

I had to agree with him.

I went on to tell him about my classes. "In the tea culture classes I learned that there are many kinds of tea: green, oolong, red tea, black tea, white tea, yellow tea and flower tea."

"This sounds interesting. Meena, I don't know much about Chinese tea but I think I may know someone who might help you and have connections. We can talk more about it. Now tell me about yourself. How were things in California? I assume your aunt and uncle kept a strict eye on you? No boys?"

"Well," I replied slowly. "There were no boys in California but something did happen on my trip back home. It's really not a big deal."

"Tell me anyway," he said.

I hesitated, even though I had known Mac most of my life and trusted him completely. My encounter with Raj seemed like it had happened a long time ago and somehow unimportant. I looked across at my friend and into his blue eyes. He had been a friend and confidant for a long time and so I shrugged and continued to speak.

"On my trip here I was traveling with a lot of things, including my backpack, trench coat and a box of tea and it was really hard to juggle it all on the airport shuttle in Singapore. But I had some help," I said looking up into his blue eyes, blushing. "There was this man, who carried the box to the airport for me."

"What? Like a porter?" Mac asked with a mischievous twinkle in his eye.

"Mac," I said. "Don't tease. He was a just fellow traveler. He had traveled quite a bit and knew a place where you could rent lockers and take a hot shower. He also bought me a coffee and we talked. Just talked."

"Ah, I knew a young man was involved. Does this man have a name?"

"Raj," I said. "Raj Kumar. He lives in Bombay and works for his father."

Mac looked taken aback for a moment and I wondered if I had shocked him with this story.

"He was a perfect gentleman," I said.

"Well, he sounds like a nice lad. Now, how about we take a walk to the green house and see the herbs I have planted," he suggested.

I followed him outside and down the garden path.

Dusk was falling but the air was warm and fragrant in the greenhouse and I immediately saw the Italian herbs he was growing. Bright green basil, oregano and thyme were sprouting in their own beds.

"I was going to use these to make a sauce," Mac said. "Look at these beauties."

He was pointing to several tomato vines, laden with bright red fruit.

"I also have garden garlic and onions and of course some capsicum peppers."

I was delighted, "You have everything to make a great marinara sauce."

"Maybe you could show Mala how to cook it," Mac said.

Mala was a little reluctant to let me into her kitchen but Mac wouldn't take no for an answer. Soon I had her chopping onions and peppers. I sliced the garlic into the thinnest slivers possible and chopped a generous handful of fresh herbs. The kitchen soon started to smell like an Italian home. Mala parboiled the tomatoes and removed the skin. I showed her how to get rid of the seeds. Mala had found a package of Indian vermicelli and I set about cooking it. Soon the pasta was ready and drained it and added a bit of ghee to keep the thin strands from sticking together. Mala opened a can of cheese and I placed slices of the cheese in the bubbling sauce until they melted into puddles of creaminess. We toasted bread on the griddle. Meanwhile Mala had cut some green beans and I quickly sautéed them in hot sesame oil and then added a generous amount of garlic.

"That is a lot of garlic," Mala said.

"I know, it looks like a lot but it will taste delicious," I assured her.

When the beans were tender, but still crunchy, I removed them from the pan and held one up for Mala to taste. She nibbled on it very tentatively and then quickly took another bite, looking surprised as she swallowed the mouthful.

"This is wonderful," she said taking another bean. "Who would have thought that beans, oil, garlic and sea salt could be so tasty and easy to make."

I smile at her, pleased with her reaction. She shooed me out of the kitchen and said she would bring a tray into the library.

I joined Mac who was sitting by a roaring fire, reading a book.

"Now this is a lovely sight," I said walking into the cozy room.

Mac looked up and smiled, "How did it work?"

"Your produce was wonderful. The vermicelli is thin but I think it will be fine with the fresh sauce."

It was a relaxing evening and I forgot all about Suresh, Dev and our bank loan.

"Tomorrow morning, I'm going to take you for a ride," Mac said, getting up and emptying the contents of his pipe into the fire.

Just then Mala came in to take the dirty dishes back to the kitchen.

"Mala, show Meena our guest room. And make sure there are clean towels and a bathrobe for her.

"Really, Master Mac," Mala sniffed. "She is not my first guest, you know."

Mac laughed as I followed Mala down the hallway.

"Good night, Mac."

"Sleep well, lass."

As I slid into bed, my toes touched the hot water bottle Mala had placed in the bed. I sighed with pleasure and fell asleep.

CHAPTER 32
MEENA

RIDING WITH MAC

I woke up to a gentle tapping. Mala entered the room with a mug of steaming tea in one hand and some folded laundry in another hand.

"Breakfast is in the dining room, anytime you are ready," she said. "I hope you slept well. Here are your clothes. They are not washed, but are air-dried by the fire. It's the best I could do."

I sat up and took the mug from her and took a sip of the delicious tea.

"Oh, thank you, Miss Mala. I slept very well and the hot water bottle in the bed was so nice and warm."

"See you soon," she said, closing the bedroom door behind her.

I finished the tea and climbed out of the bed. I had worn one of Mac's pajama tops and quickly changed into my jeans and shirt. I pulled my arms through the heavy sweater and put on my running shoes.

Mac was already finishing his breakfast.

"Ah, there you are, lass. Sleep alright?"

"Yes, I did, Mac, I fell asleep as soon as my head touched the pillow. Thank you for everything last night."

"Think nothing of it, lass. Now eat up."

Mala came in with a fresh pot of tea.

"How about some eggs, Meena?" she asked.

"I'm still full from all the pasta from last night's dinner," I said. "Just toast for me."

"Toast and marmalade coming right up," she said.

As soon as I finished my last bite of toast, Mac was ready to go.

"It's good you are wearing some walking shoes," he said. "We are going for a ride in my Jeep."

I followed him out of the house and to waiting vehicle.

"Let's go."

His driver, Ramji, was standing beside the Jeep.

"We're going on rough terrain so I thought the Jeep might be best," Mac said.

We climbed into the back and soon the jeep took off. It was too noisy to talk in the Jeep and so I didn't ask him where we were going. I guess I would see where we were headed soon enough.

We entered Mac's tea estate and bounced along on a dirt path that was liberally sprinkled with large stones and rocks. I could feel my teeth chattering against each other and I held onto the straps on the roof for dear life. After a very rocky thirty- minute drive we reached a plateau and the Jeep came to a stop, stirring up a whirlwind of dust from beneath its wheels.

"We have to walk a bit from here," Mac said. "But it's not far."

"Anything is better than being bounced in the jeep," I replied.

Mac chuckled.

"Where are we going?" I finally asked the question that was burning inside me.

"This is the southernmost part of my estate. A few years back I leased it to an investment firm" Mac answered.

I was surprised to learn that he was willing to have someone else on his beloved land.

"Well. The man was very persuasive and I knew I would benefit from what he wanted to do."

I was about to ask what he meant when we reached the end of the path where the entire slope was terraced and planted with vines. The plants were unattended, most of them withering and dried.

"Mac, what is this?"

"About four years ago, just after you left for the U.S., I had a friend come and talk to me about growing something different here. He thought grapes would be a good investment but we both later learned the hard way that the soil and mostly the climate here are not good for grapes. We left the vines to wilt. I have been waiting to clear out this slope and plant something else. Perhaps this would be the ideal place to grow a different kind of tea."

"Mac, this is what my mother invested in? These grape vines?"

Mac shook his head, "That was a mistake on my part. You know, Meena, I would have never asked her to be part of this new venture if I had known she was hurting for cash. I can't tell you how sorry I am."

"I know, Mac."

"I promise to make this right, Meena."

"I trust you, Mac," I said simply.

We walked down the hillside. The views here were breathtaking and I took a sniff of the earthy smell of soil. I noticed that the area was crisscrossed with thin black rubber hoses. Curious, I bent down to look.

"These provide drip irrigation," Mac said. "It was costly investment but we thought it would use less water in the long term. This is the perfect climate for tea. We'll pull out the vines and plant Chinese tea. If that is what you want."

I tried to imagine the whole hillside carpeted in green. Tea was Mahagiri's gold.

"Yes," I said taking a deep breath. "I would love to see Chinese tea plants growing on this hillside."

Mac laughed. "I'm so relieved to hear you say that, Meena. I think you have a good idea here about serving Chinese tea and opening a tea house. I would like to support you in this endeavor. I also mentioned my investor friend and I think he will be interested in this too. I will contact him and let you know. I have a hunch it will work out for you."

I hoped so.

"Meena, let's take you back home. Are you ready to face your mother?"

I nodded and soon we were bouncing back to Mac's house. Ramji made the turn onto the main road toward my house.

As he pulled up to the gate, I could see a mass of people crowding our front yard and blocking the gate. As soon as Ramji stopped the jeep, Mac and I rushed out. I was worried that something had happened to my mother or the twins. The last time a crowd had gathered in front of our house was because my father had died. Had someone else died?

CHAPTER 33
RAJ

Work kept Raj busy for next couple of weeks. When he finally had a free weekend he decided to visit his friend Ashwin. Ashwin had been a close friend for many years and owned an apartment in the beach town of Goa. Getting on the plane brought back memories of another plane ride and of Meena. But Raj was careful not to dwell on those thoughts. His friend was waiting for him at the airport and soon he was seated behind Ashwin on his black motorcycle.

"It's been a long time since we spent time together," Ash said as they got off the motorcycle. "You've been a stranger."

"Yeah, sorry about that," Raj replied. "But my father has kept me busy."

"So let's get our swim trunks and head to the beach. I hear from my houseboy that a tour bus has arrived." He laughed. "German girls like to go topless."

For some reason Raj wasn't thrilled with the idea as Ashwin. He was relieved to find the beach nearly empty. The men spread out beach towels and lay down.

"So how was your recent trip to the US?" Ash asked. "Any kiss and tell stories to share?"

"When have I ever shared those kinds of stories?"

"Never," Ash admitted. "But I thought I'd ask. Maybe today will be the day," Ash grinned at him.

It was hard to stay angry with Ashwin. He was just too good-natured.

"What about you? Aren't you terrorizing all the young women in Madras?"

"Hey, Madras women are safe from me. Did I tell you my parents are arranging my marriage?"

"What? You are ready to settle down?"

"Are you kidding me? Of course not, but I don't have a choice. They want me settled so that my sister can get married."

"How about that? The playboy is finally going to be tied down."

"Hey, no one is tying me down. I'm just going through the motions."

"Then why do it? Either you are committed or you're not."

"Who made you police of manners and decorum? This isn't the Raj I knew and loved."

"Maybe that Raj didn't know anything."

Ashwin sat up and leaned on his elbow. He lifted his sunglasses and looked at his friend with a mischievous gleam in his eyes, "Why, you naughty rascal! You have a girlfriend now, don't you?"

Raj rolled over onto his side, "No, there's no one. Well, there is someone but nothing definite."

"Do tell."

"Nothing to tell. I met a girl at the airport in Singapore we kind of liked each other."

"At the airport? How romantic. What's her name?"

"I'm not giving out any information. She's really no one. I probably won't ever see her again."

Ashwin lay back down on the beach towel.

"You've become so boring Raj, Even your romantic stories are dull. You have become such a stick in the mud. Remember the fun we had at UCLA?"

Raj did. But mostly he remembered that Ashwin had more fun than he did.

"Yeah, but you were the playboy, not me."

"True," Ashwin sighed. "I miss those days, bro. Carefree and doing what we wanted. Now, I am tied down by a job and traditions."

"I guess this is what growing up means," Raj said.

"Not cool at all," Ash added. "If I get married I expect a huge bachelor party."

Raj laughed, "Anything for a party for the Ash."

"Laugh if you want. I have to go see this girl soon. But I figure the trip alone will be worth it, like a mini-vacation."

"Where are you going?"

"The resort town of Mahagiri."

Raj's heart was pounding so hard he wondered if Ashwin could hear the beats. He was quiet for a long moment.

There was no way it could be Meena. The coincidence was too much.

"Do you know the girl's name?"

"Not yet. Details including photos are coming soon, I think. I wasn't paying much attention to my mother."

Raj went through the rest of the day as if he were in a trance. He counted the hours until he could get back to Bombay. He knew he had to talk to his mother. Time to confess. He just hoped he wasn't too late.

He couldn't wait for the weekend to come to an end. He knew Ash was upset with him but Raj didn't care. From the moment he heard his friend was going to Mahagiri to see a girl, he had been sure it was Meena and he had been fighting an urge to rush home. That night on the uncomfortable sofa bed in Ash's apartment he had finally come to terms with the fact that he wanted to see Meena. Heck, who was he trying to kid? He more than wanted her. He wanted to marry her.

When the visit was finally over, he couldn't have been happier to get on the tiny plane. He was one of those annoying passengers who stood up as the plane taxied down the runway.

He ignored the reproachful looks from the pretty airline stewardess and stalked out of the plane as soon as the doors were flung open. He found Dinesh waiting for him at the front entrance of the airport.

"Let's go," he said, in an abrupt tone.

He got in the front seat and caught a glimpse of Dinesh's expression.

"Sorry," he said. "I'm in a rush to get home to speak to my mother."

"Your mother is at the temple," Dinesh replied. "Are you all right?"

Dinesh had known him all his life.

"You are upset?"

Raj sighed. "It's nothing. I just need to talk to my mother. Do you know when she'll be back?"

"She is usually back by lunch time."

Raj looked at his watch. It was well past noon. "Are you supposed to pick her up?"

"No, she was going to get a ride from a friend because I had to pick you up."

"Okay. Let's just get home, then."

Dinesh didn't say anything and Raj settled back in the seat even though sitting still was hard.

Dinesh had barely stopped the car before Raj was out. He was nearly at the front door when he came back to the car.

"Sorry Dinesh, I'm in a hurry."

"I would have never guessed," Dinesh said, with a smile.

Raj nodded and walked up the steps and into the house.

He let out a breath of relief when he heard his mother's voice in the dining room. She and her father were having a cup of tea.

"Dad, Mom," he greeted them. "Do you think I could talk to you for a minute?"

"You sound so serious, Raj," his father said with a laugh.

"Would you like a cup of tea?" his mother asked.

"Not right now, Ma. I really need to talk to you for just a moment."

Raj pulled out a chair and sat down, facing his parents who were looking at him with expectant looks on their faces.

His mother raised eyebrows. "So what is the matter?"

Suddenly Raj was at a loss for words. He ran his hands through his hair and looked down at his feet.

"Just spit it out, son," his father urged.

"Okay," he said taking a deep breath. "I met this girl at the airport when I was coming home from the US. Her name is Meena and I think I might want to marry her."

His mother sat back in her chair with a comical surprised look on her face. But his father leaned forward, resting his elbows on the table.

"Did you say her name was Meena?" he asked.

But his wife interrupted him with a question. "I don't understand. A girl? The airport?"

Raj gestured a little impatiently.

"It's a simple thing to understand. I met a girl who was carrying a lot of stuff and I sort of helped her. Then she had a long wait for a connecting flight and so we talked for a bit."

"Slow down, son," his mother suggested. "You talked a while and then you promised to marry her?"

"I didn't promise her anything, Ma," he said, his voice rising with frustration. "I told you we just talked and I liked her and I think she liked me too."

"You think she liked you?" his mother sounded bewildered. "So how do you go from talking to marrying?"

"And her name is Meena? Are you sure?" his father asked again.

"Yes, yes," he muttered. He looked up at his parents.

He was getting frustrated with himself because he couldn't understand what was happening and he couldn't explain it satisfactorily to them.

"I just want you to contact her parents and say I'm interested in marrying her."

His mother stared at him as if he had spouted wings or horns. It would have been comical if it wasn't so damn important.

"I just want you to get in touch with her," he said. "Please, Ma, it's important you do it quickly."

"Why? Did something happen between the two of you?"

"Oh Lord, no." He looked so appalled that his mother's face relaxed. "I just learned that Ash was going to look at a girl in Mahagiri soon and I think it might be Meena."

His mother kept looking at him. "You realize all this sounds quite fantastic, don't you?"

He nodded, "I know, but I need you to get in touch with her parents, so they don't accept Ash's proposal."

"Really Raj, this is out of the blue. I'm not sure this is a good idea. I..."

His father placed his hand on her arm and she stopped in mid-sentence to look at him in surprise.

"I need to talk to you, Shusheela," he said. "It's really important."

"Can't your conversation wait?" Raj asked. "This matter is urgent and you really need to get in touch with Meena's parents as soon as possible."

His father looked at him and said a little impatiently, "Raj, can you please give your mother and me a moment? We need to talk."

"Why, Dad?"

"This is a private matter and I need to discuss it with your mother."

"Does it concern Meena?"

His father shook his head. "Just give us a moment."

Raj got up and left the room with a confused look on his face.

Shusheela sat back down and reached for Nandan's hand. His head was bowed down and his whole body was shaking.

"What is going on, Baba? You are scaring me. Are you ill?"

Her husband looked up at her and she then saw he was laughing.

"You are starting to alarm me, husband," Shusheela said. She attempted to pull her hand back but Nandan took it in both of his.

"You are not going to believe this, Shusheela," he said, gasping for breath. He burst out laughing again.

"Alright," Shusheela said. "I'm losing patience here."

"Remember the family I told you about in south India? The one whose spice farm I bought?"

Shusheela nodded with an unsure look on her face.

"Well, that family lives in Mahagiri and I met Meena who was getting ready to go off to college in America."

Shusheela looked at her husband, still puzzled.

"And?"

"And, I think she is the one Raj is talking about right now."

It finally clicked for Shusheela and she made a big O with her lips.

"That's why you were laughing. At the coincidence of the entire thing."

"Yes. I really liked the girl. She was smart and very pretty. I even thought at the time she would be perfect for Raj. But can you imagine his reaction if I told him I wanted him to marry this girl?"

Shusheela started to laugh. Both husband and wife couldn't stop laughing. Finally Shusheela stopped and dabbed her eyes with the end of her sari. "So shall we tell him?"

Nandan paused and thought for a moment. "Let's not tell him anything. I will call Mac and see what's what and then we can decide."

"What shall I tell him now? You can see how upset the boy was."

"You can make up some story," Nandan got up and walked out of the kitchen.

He nearly ran into Raj who was standing just by the doorway.

"So Dad, what's going on?"

"Your mother will look into the girl and let you know," his father said, not stopping to talk.

Raj walked into the kitchen. "Ma, what was that all about? What did Dad say to you?"

His mother had a strange expression on her face, "Sit down, son." His mother indicated a chair. "Your father and I are glad you want to get married. But we'll have to look into this girl's background and family before deciding anything."

"Ma, I told you she's great," Raj said.

"I'm sure she is, son, but that is not the way we do things. Now, if you want to get married to this 'great' girl, then you will have to do it my way. This means you will have to be patient."

Raj wanted to protest but his mother's firm tone meant she wasn't going to listen to his arguments.

"Alright," he muttered. "We'll do it your way."

Raj just hoped it wouldn't be too late. He left the room with a deep frown on his face. If he had looked back he would have been puzzled to see his mother's smug and satisfied smile.

CHAPTER 34
MEENA

VILLAGERS TO THE RESCUE

Dread squeezed my heart. What if my mother had died? My last conversation with her was a yelling match. I shoved my way through the crowd, Mac was right behind me.

"What's going on?" I roughly grabbed the shoulder of a man standing in front of me. He turned around and I saw that it was Raman, our cowhand.

"Raman, what is going on? Is my mother okay?"

"She's fine, Meenakutty."

I sighed in relief.

"So why is everyone gathered here?"

Raman shrugged his shoulder, "Yesterday Bhojan came to my house and told me to bring as many villagers as I could find. He told me that Little Mother needed our help and to bring money with us. So I'm here."

Raman was married to Bhojan's daughter Kashi. Before Kashi married Raman, she had been my playmate and part-time nanny to the twins.

I wanted to ask Raman more questions but Mac was urging me to keep moving. The crowd of villagers was so dense we didn't make it too far but up ahead I saw a small cement bench. The bench was under a scraggly poinsettia tree and one of my favorite spots in the front yard. There were a couple of boys standing on it but they moved over to make room for me and

Mac. I helped Mac up and then climbed up beside him. Now I could see over the heads of all the people. The crowd was noisy. I saw many familiar faces in the crowd. My friend Kumari's parents, the Sens, were there along my mother's friend Anjali and countless others who worked in our orchards, vegetable gardens or lived nearby. It seemed like the entire village of Mahagiri was here. But I didn't understand why.

Bhojan was standing on the porch steps. He raised his hands and some of the villagers close to him stopped chattering. He cleared his throat and said something.

"We can't hear you," a voice yelled.

Police constable Rohan, a family friend, pushed his way to Bhojan and handed him a bull horn. Bhojan accepted it and looked like he wasn't sure what to do with it. Then Rohan whispered something in his ear and Bhojan nodded and raised the bull horn to his mouth.

"Friends, family and neighbors," his voice sounded squeaky but the horde was silent now. Even the men sitting on the stone wall, on the farthest edge of our property, were quiet.

"I asked you all to come here…"

He paused when he heard the front door open. My mother walked out and came to an abrupt stop on the topmost step when she saw the crowd. The twins were behind her, peering out the half-open doorway. I could see Muthi and Devi standing right behind them. My mother's expression darkened as she saw the assembly of familiar faces. I knew that look. She was angry, very angry.

She walked down two more steps and stood next to Bhojan and said something to him in a low voice. He shook his head. My mother grabbed the bull horn from Bhojan and turned to the assembled villagers.

"Bhojan made a mistake. Thank you for coming but you can all go back home because I'm fine. My family is fine and there is no need for you all to worry. Please go home."

Her voice was firm and I could hear the suppressed anger in her words. She handed the bull horn back to Bhojan and went up the steps. She pulled the twins inside and slammed the front door behind her. The crowd had been quiet while she was on the steps but then a murmur rose from the crowd and grew louder as if a wave was moving through the yard. Soon some of the villagers started to push their way out, trying to leave our yard.

But Bhojan raised the bull horn, "Please don't leave."

Those who were about to leave, turned around and I could see some of them looked surprised. One man shouted, "Why should we stay? Little Mother has spoken. She says she doesn't need our help."

Bhojan spoke out, "Listen to me. Two years ago all of Mahagiri was hit by a drought. Many of us lost cattle or goats or even our land. We all struggled. Many of you came to Little Mother for help. Do you remember what she did? Do you recall, Hanni? Didn't she help you buy medicine for your sick daughter? Mada, did you lose your job in the vegetable garden? Dhooma, where did you get money to pay for a wife?"

From my perch on the stone bench I could see the people Bhojan named and all of them nodded in agreement.

"I call on these names to remind you that Little Mother never said no to us in our need. She borrowed money during the hard times and used the land and house as collateral. Now the bank wants the money back."

"Why?" a man asked. "Why are they asking for the money back?"

"The bank was sold to a man named Suresh and his company wants Little Mother to pay off her loan in full."

Bhojan fumbled with his coat pocket and pulled out a thick wad of money and held it up.

"Here's my contribution. How many of you will join me and help Little Mother?"

One of the tea pickers, a woman named Peeri, walked over to Bhojan and placed a wicker basket in front of him. The wicker basket, with a wide cotton strap, was used by tea-leaf pickers. It was usually slung around the back with the straps tied around the shoulder to keep the basket in place and so that the laborers had their hands free to pick the tender tea leaves. Bhojan looked at the basket with a questioning look on his face. Peeri untied the end of her sari and took out a handful of coins and crumpled rupee notes and threw them in the empty tea basket. They made a dull clicking sound as they fell to the bottom of the basket. Bhojan smiled and tossed his wad of cash into the basket.

I watched in amazement as laborers, villagers and friends pushed their way to the basket to share their few rupees with my mother. My heart was overflowing with love for these kind friends. Just as I was thinking I needed to get down and make my way to Bhojan, the front door abruptly opened and mother walked out. She stood on the top step and looked around at the crowd and then at the basket which was now filling up with money. She didn't look angry anymore. Her face looked like she was about to cry.

She walked down to Bhojan and gently took the bull horn from him.

"I apologize to you all," her voice was rough with unshed tears and all the villagers stopped moving. It was quiet and my mother's voice could be heard by everyone. "I was wrong to turn away your help. I am touched by your generosity and caring. I'm not sure I deserve such love but I accept your help and my family thanks you."

She couldn't go on because she was crying. My mother never wept in public and seeing her breakdown, I sobbed along with her. Mac put his arm around me.

"Your mother is something else, lass," he whispered in my ear.

I nodded.

The mass of villagers muttered among themselves and I saw more than one woman, and even a couple of men, wipe their eyes. A commotion from the front of the house made all of us turn and look in that direction. A car door slammed and from my high vantage point I saw Suresh and Dev make their way through the horde. They pushed their way and Suresh came to an abrupt stop in front of my mother. He fixed his jacket and patted down his hair. I couldn't see his expression but I could see my mother wipe her eyes and look at Suresh with suspicion and distrust.

"Why are you here, Suresh?" her voice was cold and unwelcoming. Everyone could hear her clearly because it was so quiet.

Suresh laughed a little nervously, "I received a message to come here after 1 o' clock."

My mother had a puzzled look on her face but Bhojan stepped up, "Little Mother, I asked Mr. Suresh to come here because I and the rest of Mahagiri had something to tell him."

Bhojan picked up the bull horn and addressed the crowd, ignoring Suresh and Dev.

"These are the two men who were threatening to take away Little Mother's home. I wanted everyone to see them for who they really are."

"This is man who wanted to throw Little Mother out on the street?" a laborer asked. He walked up with a menacing stride. I couldn't see his face but I'm sure he looked threatening because Suresh and Dev took a step back. The man pulled out a small knife, one that was used to cut tea leaves. It was small but very sharp. At the sight of the knife, Suresh hastily made his way up the porch steps.

The man and the crowd pressed forward. Bhojan put his body between the crowd and Suresh and Dev.

"Stop, Dhooma. There is no need for violence."

Bhojan pushed the men back and turned to Suresh.

"Here is your money."

I saw Suresh's surprised look at he eyed the wicker basket, now overflowing with cash.

"Yes," Bhojan said. "Little Mother is part of our village and we take care of our own. Take your money and leave."

Suresh patted his forehead with a handkerchief. He glanced back at the crowd and then at my mother.

"Little Mother," he started to say.

"Don't call me that. Only my friends and family can use that title," my mother told him.'

I could see Suresh swallow and nod, "Mrs. Unnikrishanan, I'm sorry. I have no wish to distress you."

"You better not," a man shouted waving a larger knife.

Suresh looked terrified for a moment and then patted his hair once again and said in a smooth voice, "Please, there is no need to re-pay the loan right now. I was wrong to even ask you to do that. It was a terrible mistake on my part. Please forgive me."

My mother didn't say anything for a long moment.

"Suresh, I have no wish to do any kind of business with you but these people need jobs. So I'm asking you to make sure you use local laborers and workers in the resort you are building."

"I promise Little…Mrs. Unnikrishanan," Suresh said eagerly. "I promise to pay fair wages too."

"Well, that's settled then," my mother said. "You may leave."

The crowd parted and let the two men leave. They kept their heads down and hurried out the front gate. The mass of villagers urged them forward with insults and taunts.

My mother had the bull horn in her hand, "Everyone, please let the men go in peace. Now, I have only one more thing to say. This money we have gathered today doesn't belong to me or my family. It belongs to Mahagiri. We need a new school and this will pay for it. Now everyone, please go home. I will never forget your generosity and you know you can always come here if you need anything."

The crowd cheered and I could hear mutterings of "Bless you, Little Mother."

Once the crowd started dispersing, I jumped off the bench and helped Mac down. We made our way to the porch where my mother was saying good-bye.

She smiled when she saw me. I hugged her tightly. We both turned, our arms still around each other's waist, and looked at Mac.

"Sudha, you are a wonder," Mac said. "Never a dull moment here."

"Mac, thank you for bringing Meena back home."

"It was my pleasure. I want to talk to you in private, Sudha. Can I call you later?"

"Of course, Mac."

"Take care of yourself, lass. I'll be seeing you soon."

My mother and I turned and walked up the porch steps.

"I'm sorry, Amma," I said.

"Oh Meena, no need for you to be sorry. I was so worried I forgot what really mattered. I would never make you do something you didn't want to."

"Still…."

"No, Meena. I promise, no more seeing ceremonies for you."

I laughed out in relief and my mother hugged me close and laughed along with me.

Little did I know she was going to break that promise, very soon.

CHAPTER 35
MEENA

MOVING FORWARD

The next day Mac called, asking to speak to my mother. I couldn't help myself as I stood behind the living room door, eaves dropping on the conversation.

"Yes, Mac. What? That is amazing news. She didn't tell me anything."

I could hear only my mother's end of the conversation and she seemed confused and happy at the same time. When she finished I stepped out into the hallway. "Amma, what is going on with Mac? What did he want?"

"What?" she asked. She looked a little distracted. "Meena, I can't talk right now. I have something I need to discuss with Muthi."

She hurried off toward the kitchen and I went onto the front porch and sat on the cement stoop. The bougainvillea vines on either side of the doorway were in full bloom and I stared blindly at their vivid colors. What was going on? I didn't like secrets, especially secrets kept from me. They were usually not pleasant like the one involving Suresh.

The next morning while I was sipping my coffee, I casually asked Muthi, "So, Muthi. Did Amma talk to you last night? You know, about that important matter?"

Muthi stopped pouring hot milk in the coffee; the steel pitcher paused in mid-air. "Now, what matter are you talking about, Meena?"

I swallowed a mouthful of hot coffee, "Uh, you know the secret matter between Amma and Mac?"

Muthi smiled sweetly, "I have no idea what you are talking about, kutty. Can you please take this cup of coffee to Devi? She is in the front yard."

I took the cup but knew she too was keeping something from me.

CHAPTER 36
RAJ

WAITING

When you are in a hurry, it seems like the entire world slows to a snail's pace. He had been unable to eat or sleep and thought some physical exercise would help. The ground was wet and muddy but it felt good to be outside and move around. The rains had let up for the hour he had been jogging. But just as he came up the driveway, the sky opened up and the warm monsoon rains poured down. After a cool shower he felt a bit better.

He went downstairs to find his mother in the kitchen with the matchmaker. Karuna was not related to them but had a reputation of being a matchmaker. In the past Raj had assiduously avoided her whenever she visited because he wanted to have nothing to do with her. Now he was hoping she would come by with her package of horoscopes and photos of eligible girls, or at least of one particular girl.

They were sipping tea and Karuna was munching on biscuits. He picked up a banana and poured himself a glass of cold water before joining them at the table.

Karuna looked at him with a critical eye, "You have lost weight, Raj," she muttered. "Too much running around and not enough curry and chapattis."

"Nice to see you, Karuna aunty," Raj replied. "Did you get Mother's message?"

"Yes, I did. Why such an interest in this girl?"

Raj shrugged, "I just heard about her from a friend. So were you able to contact her?"

Karuna regarded him with shrewd eyes. "Not yet," she said. "I've put out feelers to my friend in Mahagiri and she will go visit the family and talk to them."

"Can't you just call them up and...?"

Karuna interrupted him, "There is a certain protocol to all this. You can't just barge in and upset the apple cart."

What cart? What was this infernal woman talking about?

He reigned in his frustration and tried to talk calmly, "Can I see her paperwork?"

Karuna pushed a sheet of paper toward him. There wasn't much information except he saw what he thought was a phone number. He stared at the number trying hard to memorize it.

As if guessing what he was up to, Karuna snatched the paper back from him.

"Do not think of contacting them yourself," she warned. "That is not how it is done."

"Then you call them from our phone and tell them you have another interested party."

Karuna exchanged a glance with Raj's mother.

"You always told me," Karuna said to Shusheela. "That your boy wasn't ready for marriage."

"I had thought that too," Shusheela admitted. "But he has been like this for the past couple of days. He wants to contact this girl and I thought it was best to call you."

"You were right to do that," Karuna said. "All right since the boy is so eager, I will contact the Mahagiri matchmaker at once. I will come by in a couple of days."

More waiting. Raj thought to himself.

CHAPTER 37
MEENA

SURPRISES

I had just finished a jog around the orchards and was sipping on a glass of water in the dining room when I heard the sound of voices in the living room. There was the distinct murmur of women's voices, along with the occasional deep rumble of a man.

I was curious so I walked down the hallway and peered into the living room. I clutched the water glass in one hand and slowly pushed open the door. The formal living room with its fireplace matching sofa and chairs was used only on special occasions when we were entertaining important guests. Who could my mother be entertaining today? I was taken aback to see my mother, Muthi, matchmaker aunty and Mac, all sitting and laughing together. I had stumbled on a very strange and cozy gathering.

"Mac?" I called out before I could stop myself.

"Meena." He struggled out of the sofa. "I was just here visiting with your mother."

I nodded and looked at matchmaker aunty who snorted and said, "I was just passing by and your mother invited me to tea."

I entered the room and looked down at the coffee table which was strewn with papers. I picked up a piece. It was my horoscope.

"What's going on?" I asked looking at the group seated on the sofa in front of me, "Why are you looking at my horoscope?"

My mother sighed and stood up and came toward me. She tried to put an arm around my shoulder but I shrugged it off.

"Meena, it is not what you are thinking."

"Oh, and what am I thinking, Amma?" I couldn't help feeling hurt.

I turned to Mac, "I thought you were my friend. What are you doing here with my horoscope?"

My mother and Mac exchanged looks.

"Let's go outside, Meena," Mac said. "Your mother and I have something to tell to you."

It was warm and bright in the sunshine. But I didn't find the beauty to be enjoyable at all. I wanted answers from my mother and Mac. We walked in silence to the side garden and to the bench by the Pooja garden. Mac sat down and placed his cane on the edge of the bench. My mother indicated to me to join them. I shook my head. I preferred to stand.

"Meena," Mac began. He then cleared his throat. "A friend of a friend approached me with a marriage proposal."

I started to speak but he held up his hand, "Wait, let me finish. This boy is a really good match and I brought the proposal to your mother. We were just discussing it when you walked in. We had not decided on marrying you off or doing anything you didn't want."

My mother looked up at me with gentle eyes, "Meena, I have already promised you I wouldn't marry you off. Can you please trust me?"

I didn't say a word. Instead I stared at both of them and then I slowly nodded.

"All right. So what were you all discussing?"

Mac and my mother again exchanged looks.

"Well, the plan is for you to come meet someone."

I wanted to interrupt, but Mac held up a hand and continued. "Nothing formal, just tea at my house."

"This sounds like a seeing ceremony to me," I said. I was starting to get more and more upset. Would my mother never give up?

"Please listen, Meena," My mother said. "Just come and meet this young man and his family."

Mac added, "We promise we won't make you do anything you don't want to."

"Then why go through this whole farce?"

"Please, as a favor to an old man," Mac said in a wheedling tone.

"Oh, now you are pulling the old man card? Mac, that is a low blow."

I thought for a long moment. Mac and my mother looked at me with hopeful expressions on their faces. They looked like children longing for a present.

"Alright," I finally said. "But since this is not a seeing ceremony, I don't want to dress up in a sari. No interview? No questions asked?"

Again Mac and my mother exchanged a look, a secret, almost guilty one.

"Agreed," my mother said. "But Meena, you will wear something presentable, won't you? Not your running clothes?"

I pretended to think.

"No running clothes but I won't wear makeup or flowers in my hair," I said firmly. "I get to choose what I wear whether it is a sari or a pair of jeans."

Mac stood up and grabbed his cane.

"So I'll be in touch."

My mother and Mac started walking down the path back to the house.

"Wait," I called out. "One more thing. If this whole farce doesn't work you two will finally give up on the idea of marrying me off, right? And I get to work on the tea house idea?"

My mother came back toward me, "Meena, I have always wanted your happiness and this time is no different. I promise I will not force you into anything. Will you believe me?"

I nodded and sat down on the bench.

"Aren't you coming?" Mac asked, looking over his shoulder at me.

"I will," I said. "Give me a moment."

I watched the two of them walk away, their heads together discussing something. I don't know why I agreed to this ceremony or tea or whatever they wanted to call it. Why did I get the feeling that Mac and my mother were not telling me the truth? Something was going on. Perhaps Thangam could do some spying for me.

CHAPTER 38
RAJ IS SURPRISED

"Son, please come here for a moment," Shusheela called out.

Raj had been on his way to the office but he turned back and went inside. His parents were in the living room, waiting for him.

"We have some news for you," his mother said. She indicated he sit down.

"Yes?" Raj asked, as he sat on the edge of the chair.

"Well, we and Kavitha tried our best to contact the girl in Mahagiri," his mother said.

"Her name is Meena." Raj said firmly

"Yes, yes," his father said. "We haven't had any success but my friend Mac lives in Mahagiri."

"I remember Mac," Raj said. "Isn't he English or something?"

"Scottish," his father answered. "He has asked us to visit him and perhaps he has contacts in the area that can help us find her."

Raj looked puzzled. "Why is it such a problem to find her, I don't understand," he said.

"I think the matchmaker is having difficulty communicating with her counterpart in Mahagiri," his mother said. "So do you want to try see if Mac can help us or not?"

Raj remembered Meena mentioning her friend Mac in Mahagiri.

Raj stood up. "Let's do it."

His parents also stood up.

"So we'll leave soon as we make travel arrangements."

The next few days flew by but time couldn't pass quickly enough for Raj, who was glad to board a plane that would take them to Pellaur.

"We'll hire a taxi to take us up the hill to Mahagiri," his father said.

Raj agreed to all the plans. He just wanted to see Meena again.

CHAPTER 39
MEENA

NOT A SEEING CEREMONY

I couldn't believe Mac and my mother had convinced me to go through yet another seeing ceremony but this time I was determined to make it happen on my terms.

"No sari. No jewelry," I told my mother.

"What will you wear instead?" Muthi asked in an indignant tone.

"Jeans and a tunic," I replied. "I want my hair loose."

"She is definitely inviting the evil spirits to this ceremony," Muthi said, shaking her head. "You know that modest girls never leave their hair loose. They braid it and wear jasmine flowers."

But her lamentations didn't change my mind and I wanted to wear what I felt comfortable in However, I was a little surprised that my mother was going along with my plans.

So here it was a week later and I was in my comfortable blue jeans and purple and white Indian tunic. My hair was held back from my face with a clip. Thangam insisted that I pin a strand of creamy jasmine blooms in my hair but there were no other ornaments or bobby pins in my hair. My hair fell in loose curls down my back. I ignored Muthi's tut-tutting as she watched me put on lipstick and eye shadow.

"No bindi? Really, kutty?"

"Alright," I agreed. "I'll wear a bindi."

"How about this simple necklace?" my mother asked. She held out a delicate gold choker, inlaid with tiny pearls, with matching earrings. I had a weakness for jewelry, gold and otherwise, and so I put on the choker and earrings.

"That's a little better," Muthi said.

I stared at my reflection in the mirror, and something reminded me of Raj. Why was I thinking of him now? I shook my head to clear it and accompanied my mother to the waiting car. We had agreed that my mother and Muthi would accompany me. Thangam was disappointed.

"But why do I have to stay home?" she asked. "I'm old enough to come too."

I looked at my mother and then at my sister's eyes which were filling rapidly with hot tears.

"All right, Thangam, you can come," I said. "Quick, go get dressed."

"I won't be long." She danced out of the hallway with a happy grin on her face.

We waited in the living room and true to her word Thangam was back quickly dressed in a dark red and yellow silk skirt and blouse. She had braided her hair and wore a dark red bindi dot.

"You look very nice, kutty," Muthi said. "More bride-like than the bride herself."

I ignored Muthi's comments. I was eager to get this over with and soon we were on our way to Mac's for tea and a seeing ceremony.

CHAPTER 40
RAJ

JOURNEY UP THE HILL

Raj sat in front with the taxi cab driver who turned out to be a chatty fellow.

"So, your first trip to Mahagiri, sir?" he asked Raj.

Raj nodded, "Yes, I hear it is beautiful."

The driver honked at a bicyclist and swerved to avoid a stray dog crossing the street.

"It is beautiful but too cold," the driver said. "I prefer Pellaur where you don't need a sweater all the time."

Raj rolled down the window and inhaled the warm air. He remembered Meena saying the air in Mahagiri was cold and crisp. He couldn't wait to experience the invigorating Mahagiri breeze.

The driver stopped talking to concentrate on the hairpin turns. Raj was content to look out the window and imagine what it would be like to see Meena again. Would she be surprised?

"Raj." His father tapped him on the shoulder. "We should stop soon so your mother and I can stretch our legs."

Raj wanted to insist they keep driving instead, he nodded and turned to the driver, "When you find a convenient stop, please pull over so my parents can walk around a bit."

"I was going to pull up in about ten minutes," the driver said. "There is a truck stop and I want to get a cup of coffee and smoke."

A few minutes later the driver pulled up alongside a tour bus. The truck stop consisted of a row of small shops selling everything from plastic buckets to packages of chips. There were vendors hawking bottles of cold drinks and hot tea. A boy was walking around selling packets of cigarettes, Indian beedis and matches. It was a surprisingly busy place alive with the smell of boiled tea, diesel fumes and rotting fruit.

Raj got out of the car, opened his mother's door and helped her out. He accompanied her to the public toilets and waited outside.

"Would you like some tea?" he asked her when she came back out.

"Yes, but I think your father would prefer coffee."

They walked back and found their father holding two glass tumblers of piping-hot tea. He offered them the tea and went back to the stall to get a cup of coffee. Raj sipped the warm, too-sweet drink and wondered what Meena was up to.

As the car made its way up the hill, the air became cooler. His mother wrapped a shawl around herself and Raj was tempted to roll up the car window. The breeze was cool and the air smelled fresh. The next leg of the journey seemed to go by quickly and soon they were pulling into Mac's driveway. The Scotsman and his dog were waiting by the front door to greet them.

Nandan made the introductions and Mac led them into his house.

"This is Miss Mala, my housekeeper," he said gesturing toward a beaming older woman.

"Welcome. I'm making a special tea for this afternoon."

"Yes, yes, that is good, Miss Mala. I'll show our guests their rooms so they can freshen up."

"Actually, do you mind if I went for a walk?" Raj asked. "I just want to stretch my legs."

"Excellent idea, my boy," Mac said. "You go ahead and we'll keep each other company."

Raj walked along the path and across the lawn. He found another path leading down the hill, winding past tea bushes. He finally came to a clearing with a large rock on one side. He stopped at the large boulder and leaned on its warm surface. He went around to the other side and was able to scramble up to the top of the gigantic rock. He stood on the smooth surface and looked down at the valley below. It was breath-taking and at that moment he understood why Meena loved this place with its fresh air, blue skies and wonderful views. He knew she was somewhere in this valley, perhaps just below him in one of the houses. He sighed and turned back toward the estate.

CHAPTER 41
MEENA'S TEA TIME

Jaibal drove us up the hill to Mac's house. No walking this time, although I would have preferred the delay a walk would have provided. We pulled into the driveway and Jaibal parked the car on the gravel. I could smell the late-blooming flowers from Mac's side garden. The lawn was pristine in the early evening sunlight. The entire place was peaceful and I felt calm after taking a few deep whiffs of the garden scents.

"Ready, Meena?" Muthi asked me.

"Ready, Muthi," I replied. I took her arm and we walked up the short driveway and, up the cement steps leading to the house. My mother and Thangam were already at the front door, waiting for us.

Thangam lifted up the heavy metal door knocker and tapped it once. I was about to tell her to do it again, when the door swung open.

It was Miss Mala, who looked at us with an astonished expression on her face.

"Little Mother," she said. "I wasn't expecting you. The master had told me we were having some visitors but I didn't....

Mala quickly gathered herself. "Never mind, come in, come in. Muthi, so good to see you and, Meena, you look beautiful."

I knew she wanted to ask us what we were doing there, but before she could say anything Mac was at her side.

"Good, good you are all here. My guests are in the library. Miss Mala, you can bring the tea in about fifteen minutes."

Mac looked at us and smiled. "Follow me."

He turned to go down the hallway. Muthi touched my mother's shoulder.

"Sudha, I'll go help Mala with the tea and join you soon."

My mother nodded and turned to me, "Come on, Meena."

I hesitated, pulling a little away from my mother. I don't know what it was but a strange feeling came over me and I felt a bit faint.

"Go on, Chechi," Thangam pushed me toward Mac who was watching me with a sympathetic look on his face.

He came toward me and took my cold hand in his warm ones. "It's going to be all right, Meena. Trust me."

I looked up into his sky-blue eyes and nodded. I did trust him and so I let him lead me into the familiar library. The door was partially open and I could hear the sound of voices. Through the crack I could see a roaring fire and the familiar chairs by the fireplace. Suddenly I felt better. This room had that effect on me. Mac pushed the door open and pulled me through into the library. It took a moment for my eyes to adjust to the light in the room. I saw an elegant looking lady seated on one of the sofas and standing behind her was a familiar face. "Is that you, Mr. Nanadan?" I asked.

I turned to Mac who was grinning at me and then around to face my mother who had a smug expression on her face.

"What are you doing here, Mr. Nandan?" I asked.

He came forward and clasped my hands in his. I remembered him clearly; after all he had bought my father's spice estate.

"It is good to see you, Meena. You are all grown up and looking beautiful."

That is when I looked over Nandan's shoulder and saw another familiar face. Raj! His face must have been a mirror expression of mine because he too looked totally shocked. He started to come toward me, stumbling over an end table and knocking it on its side so that all the knick-knacks clattered to the floor. He bent down to pick up the fallen objects. At that moment my eyes grew dim and I felt my legs give out from under me. Nandan caught me before I fell to the ground.

When I opened my eyes I was lying on the sofa with Thangam pressed close to me, stroking my arm.

"Are you all right, Chechi?" she was asking.

I tried to sit up.

"Here sip on this," my mother pressed a glass of cold water into my hands.

I took a sip and struggled again to sit upright. I looked up at the faces surrounding me, including Raj who was standing close by with a concerned expression on his face. That is when I realized he was really here and that it wasn't some trick my mind was playing on me.

"What?" I tried to ask a question but my tongue was all tied up in my dry mouth.

I took another sip of water. My mother sat down next to me. Mac pulled up a chair and sat down. Nandan also found a seat.

It was Mac who spoke, "Sorry, Meena, to play this little trick on you." His apology seemed a little false as he had a huge grin on his face. "As you know Nandan and I are old friends and he contacted me."

"Wait," I said. "I know about you and Mr. Nandan but how is." .

I couldn't quite get out Raj's name.

"Raj is my son," Nandan said in a soft tone. "He told me."

"Dad," Raj interrupted. "Let me."

He now pulled up a stool and sat beside me. I looked into those eyes, eyes I thought I would never see again and felt a bubble of hysteria welling up inside me. What was going on? How did Raj get here? Was all this a dream?

"Meena, my father is Nandan, the same man who bought your father's spice plantation. When I got back home after seeing you off I visited my friend Ash in Goa and he told me that his family was setting up his marriage to a girl in Mahagiri. He didn't know her name but I was worried it was you and that's when I knew I didn't want him to marry you."

Raj looked down at his hands. He looked up at me and smiled. "I rushed home and told my father and mother about meeting you at the airport and wanting to see you again."

His father tapped him on the shoulder, "You said you wanted to marry her, remember, Raj?"

Raj blushed and I felt an odd desire to giggle at his embarrassment. "Yes, I did say that and apparently my old man and mother along with this foreigner decided to play a trick on me."

"Now, now," Mac said with a chuckle. "Who are you calling *foreigner*? I consider myself Indian after living here for the past fifty years. We just wanted to have a little fun."

I found the whole situation intolerable. I turned to face him, "Really Mac, I came to this so-called seeing ceremony trying my best to please you and Amma. This is not funny at all."

There was silence in the room. The fire crackled merrily.

"I'm sorry," my mother spoke up. "I shouldn't have gone along with this charade. I'm sorry, kutty."

I said nothing.

"So does this mean you aren't getting married, Chechi?" Thangam asked. She sounded bewildered.

That's when it all hit me. Raj was here and wanting to marry me. Before I could say anything Mala and Muthi came in with the tea tray.

"A cuppa!" Mac exclaimed. "Just what we need."

I didn't think that was what we needed at all. Raj was staring at me and I couldn't help blushing at his intense gaze. He stood up and looked down at me, "Meena, perhaps you could walk with me?"

"But it's dark outside" Thangam said.

"That's alright," my mother said. "You two go along."

CHAPTER 42
MEENA

WALKING WITH RAJ

"I know this whole thing has been a surprise for you," Raj said as we walked down the concrete steps.

We crossed the lawn. The sun was setting behind the house and the garden was bathed in the last golden light of the day. The flower garden looked as if it had been sprinkled with saffron dust.

We paused at the path leading down the hill toward my home. I turned to Raj, but he held up a hand. "Wait, let me finish, okay? After we said good-bye at the airport, I kept thinking about you. Then when I went to visit my friend and he said his family was looking into a proposal from a girl who lived in Mahagiri. I was panicked at the thought it might be you. I realized I wanted to see you again. And yes, marry you. My parents, Mac and your mom planned this whole secret meeting. I had no idea. They didn't tell they were going to surprise you."

He stopped speaking and looked at me, "Though you really aren't dressed for a seeing ceremony, are you?"

I laughed, relief and joy starting to flow through my body, "No, when my mother wanted me to come see this mysterious boy she and Mac had picked out for me, I told them I would come but on my terms so I dressed the way I wanted."

"You are beautiful," Raj said, his voice soft and warm. "I'm sorry I made you faint."

I blushed. "I was a little tired. I've never fainted before."

I led him around the lawn to Mac's back garden. Here the fragrance of the flowers was heady. The sun was setting rapidly in the west and the world was now bathed in a pink glow.

"Meena, we had a connection at the airport and I thought...."

He stopped and turned toward me. He put his hands on my shoulder and looked down at me.

"We did," I said looking up at him. He looked as handsome as a god from a Hindu myth in the pink sunset. "I never thought I'd see you again. It has been a shock."

"But you are glad to see me?"

"Oh yes," I said with a smile. "I'm more than just glad, I'm so happy."

I was shocked when he dropped to one knee and took my hands in his, "Meena, will you please consider being my wife?"

He pulled a wine-colored velvet box out of his front pocket.

"I bought this while I was waiting to hear from you," he said.

I took the jewelry box from him and opened it. Inside was a beautiful diamond and emerald ring. The stones sparkled in the setting sun. For a moment I was tongue-tied. Everything was happening so quickly.

"Of course I'll marry you, Raj," I said, dropping to my knees in front of him so that we were facing each other. "I just never thought I'd say that."

I watched Raj slip the ring onto my finger and looked at the sparkling ring.

"I never thought the day would end like this," I said, feeling a little teary-eyed. "I thought I would be saying no to an arranged marriage but instead...you came and I'm so happy I could cry."

I felt tears slipping down my cheeks. He gently brushed them away.

"I like happy tears," he said softly as he took both my hands in his.

We gazed at each other. It seemed the most natural thing to lean forward and kiss him. I sighed happily as we sat back on our heels. Raj pushed a stray curl out of my eyes and I looked down at the sparkling ring on my finger.

"Those parents of ours sure had us fooled," I said. "I'd like march in there and tell them we are not getting married. Shock my mother and Mac out of their complacency."

"You know," he said. "We really should give the old folks a heart attack."

"What are you saying?"

He grinned as he pulled me to my feet, "I have an idea. Come on and play along, okay?"

I nodded as we walked back to the house, hand in hand.

"You are really okay?" Raj asked.

"Yes," I said with a grin. "I'm fine. Better than fine—I'm great."

CHAPTER 43
TEACHING THE ELDERS
A LESSON

We let go of our hands as we approached the house.

"Slip your ring finger into your pocket," Raj said.

He looked at me, "Ready?"

I nodded.

He pushed open the door and stalked down the hallway and into the library.

"Really, Mom and Dad," he said in a loud voice. "What were you thinking? Dad? Mac?

He looked around at the stunned faces.

"What are you saying?" Mac said, getting up and leaning on his walking stick.

"I'm saying that Meena just informed me she is not going to marry me."

My mother also stood up and turned to where I was standing by the open doorway. "Meena, what does this mean? What is Raj saying?"

I swallowed and nodded, "Yes, Amma. That's right. I don't want to marry Raj. He has all kinds of old-fashioned ideas about women."

"Me? Old fashioned? What about you, Meena?" Raj asked. I could see the twinkle in his eye. "You said you had a boyfriend in California whom you want to marry."

I tried not to grin. He was good but I wasn't going to let him get away with that statement.

"Oh, yeah? You just told me you expect your wife to stay home, have children and supervise the servants."

"Wait, wait," Raj's father spoke up. "What is this? What are you two talking about? This doesn't sound like you, Raj. I thought you wanted to marry Meena?"

His mother added, "You were the one who made us find her."

Raj added. "Well, I changed my mind after seeing her again. I want a traditional wife who wears a silk sari."

"I told you, kutty," Muthi said. She couldn't keep silent any longer. "I told you to dress up."

My mother stood up. "Meena, what boyfriend? What is Raj saying?"

At this I couldn't help it—I started to laugh. Raj looked at me and started to laugh too. We laughed as our families looked at us as if we had lost our minds. After a few minutes, we stopped gasping and Raj reached over and pulled my hand out of my jean's pocket.

"We were just teasing you," he said. "She said yes."

He held up my hand so everyone could see the ring.

Muthi was indignant and said, "You two are very disrespectful."

"I'm sorry, Muthi," I said and went over to hug her.

I was introduced to Shusheela who shook her head and looked at us.

"You two deserve each other. I think you will be fine together."

My mother came to hug me. "Meena? Nandan and Mac convinced me it was all in good fun. We are even now, right?"

She looked at me searchingly and I hugged her back.

"Oh, Amma. I'm so happy."

CHAPTER 44
MEENA

PLANS

With that wedding plans began. The next day, Shusheela came over to talk to my mother about sarees, jewelry and menus. I sat with Muthi and tried to take part in all the discussions but my mind kept wandering. Finally my mother took pity of me, "Go on, Meena. Go to Mac's house and find Raj."

I thanked her and was soon on my way up the hill to Mac's home. Mala let me in and I found all three men in the living room. Raj stood up and came toward me with a huge grin. He took my hand in his.

"Meena, you are just in time. We were talking tea."

"My favorite subject," I replied with a laugh.

We walked and sat down on the sofa, still holding hands. Nandan and Mac watched us and then Mac said, "Meena, you may not know this but after Nandan bought your father's estate, he came here to visit me. He really liked Mahagiri and was open to the idea of starting a business here. I sold him the south side of my estate and he had hoped to grow grapes. Remember I showed you the abandoned vines?"

I nodded, "You said grapes can't really grow in this climate."

"Yes but now that you have come up with a different kind of tea planation; I think this business might be the right one for all of us. A tea room with a peaceful garden would be a real tourist attraction."

Nandan added, "I think this kind of development will be good for Mahagiri. I'd like to preserve area's natural beauty."

I explained the idea of tea ceremonies from China and Japan and my vision for the tea room.

"Mostly I want it to be a quiet oasis where you can come unwind with old-time service. There would be quiet gardens, stone benches and water fountains."

I glanced at Raj's father who looked intrigued by the concept. "I think those are great ideas."

Raj cleared his throat. "Yes, Meena was very enthusiastic about the Chinese tea service and the food that would be served with the tea. In fact, that is all she wanted to talk about when we first met."

I playfully dug my elbow into his side. "That's not true. I thought I talked about Mahagiri."

"You're right," he replied. "Your descriptions made me want to visit this place."

Mac interrupted us, "You know my estate would be ideal for a tea room. We could have English tea in the library and the Chinese or Japanese tea in the garden."

"It would require quite a bit of remodeling," Nandan said. "Are you up to it, Mac?"

Mac looked down at his hands which were resting on his cane.

"I didn't want to bring this up on such a special and happy day," he said.

I felt my throat tightening and my insides tensing at his words. This didn't sound like good news.

"But the truth is I'm a sick man. I have a heart condition."

He held up his hands as we all started to talk at once.

"I'm not dying yet," he said with a chuckle. "But my time is limited and I want to see you married, Meena, and the fact you are marrying my friend's son is a blessing to me. I want to see this place thriving as a tea sanctuary."

"I'm sorry, Mac," I said, tears filling my eyes. Mac leaned over and placed a warm hand over mine.

"This is not the time to grieve, Meena. There is a lot of work to be done. You and Raj have to get started on the tea business." He smiled. "There is also the marriage business."

I agreed but sadness filled my heart at the thought of losing my friend.

CHAPTER 45
A WEDDING

Long ago there was a small kingdom ruled by a kind and brave king named Janaka. He and his wife longed for a child. One day while the king was walking along a field, he heard the cries of a baby. He walked into the field and found a baby girl in the furrows. He and his wife adopted the girl and considered her a gift from the gods and named her "Sita" meaning one who was found in the earth's furrow.

Sita grew up to be a girl of great beauty and charm. When it was time for her to get married, King Janaka decided to hold a Swamyamvara. During this ceremony the bride-to-be is presented to a group of eligible men who take part in a contest to win her hand. Many eligible princes and kings attended Sita's Swamyamvara. The king possessed an immensely heavy bow given to him by none other than Lord Shiva and now King Janaka decided that whoever could lift the heavy bow and string an arrow through it could marry Sita.

It was at this time a young prince named Rama, along with his brother Lakshmana, stopped by on their way back to their kingdom. The brothers had spent time in a local hermitage helping the sage Vishwamitra. Prince Rama watched as suitor after suitor tried to lift the heavy bow. Some could lift the bow but were unable to string it. Vishwamitra urged Rama to try to string the bow and everyone was amazed when the young prince picked up and the bow and broke it as he was testing out the tautness of the bowstring. Legend has it that the sound of the bow breaking could be heard across three kingdoms.

Prince Rama was declared the winner and Sita draped a garland of flowers around his neck. The wedding of Rama and Sita was a splendid and grand affair. Rama's three brothers were also married at the same time and there was much celebration and jubilation in both kingdoms. All four couples returned to their home in Ayodhya where Prince Rama was to rule.
—As told by Muthi.

The next few months were a flurry of activity, but my joy was tempered with sadness. The more I thought about it the more I realized how much Mac meant to me. His humor, strength and Scottish commonsense made him a special friend. I enjoyed getting to know Raj's parents. I found his mother, Shusheela, to be a beautiful and cultured woman who resembled Raj. I also enjoyed renewing my acquaintance with his father Nandan, who was talkative and gregarious. I would meet his sisters at a wedding reception that was being planned in Bombay in the coming weeks.

Raj and I spent an afternoon in Lower Mahagiri at the area's only jewelry store where I found an emerald necklace with matching bracelets and earrings. He bought presents for Devi, Muthi, my mother and Thangam. Next door was a place selling watches and Raj bought some as gifts for my brother, Bhojan, Raman and Jaibal.

My mother had invited the sari vendor to our home and he spread out all the silk saris in the living room. The room smelled of fresh starch and looked like a dhobi (washerwoman) village with the yards of colorful fabric.

So exactly six months after he proposed Raj and I stood in Mac's gazebo preparing to take our wedding vows. He was dressed in a cream-colored silk kurta top with black silk pants. I was dressed in traditional Kerala robes the color of rich clotted cream intertwined with golden threads and designs. I wore Raj's gift around my neck along with countless gold chains. Mac stood next to me, leaning heavily on his cane. His brow was beaded with moisture and pain had carved deep lines into his face. He refused to sit down and insisted on standing next to me.

"You are the daughter of my heart," he said. "Giving you away on this day is what I want to do."

Over the past few days I had learned that Mac had left his house and land to Raj and me. The house would be renovated to become a small lodge where tea lovers could come and experience life on a tea plantation. There would be tours, tastings and perhaps even tea picking. It would be an interactive experience for those who visited the tea garden. But all that would come in the future. Right now, the priest was chanting prayers in Sanskrit. If I looked over the priest's head I could see Mahagiri valley spread beneath us. It was lush, fertile and beautiful. I had loved this place all my life and it was fitting that my wedding would take place beneath the blue skies on this hillside.

After the wedding we sat down for a feast prepared by Devi, Muthi, my mother and Mala who was determined to add her own touch to the meal. She had baked, with help from the local bakery, a large white wedding cake. The moist, golden cake was rich with dried fruit, and the sweet frosting had a hint of fresh lemon.

Later that evening Raj and I sat with Mac who was on the sofa in front of the fire. Raj reached for my hand. Mac stirred, "What a way to spend your wedding night."

I smiled at his dear face, "We would not be in any other place."

Raj added, "Anyway, Meena, here was just telling me about your Scottish legend of the Selkie."

Mac attempted to sit up and Raj helped him. I placed a pillow behind his back. He coughed, sounding congested. I poured him a glass of water.

"I'd prefer my tea," he grumbled as he took a sip of water.

"I'll get some," Raj said.

I sat down next to Mac. He took my hand in his. I remembered a time when his hands had seemed so big and warm. Now, they were cold and seemed to have shrunk. I clung to his cold fingers.

"Meena," he said. "I don't want to die on your wedding day. I don't want to ruin your special day forever."

"Mac, you gave me this special day. You couldn't ruin it if you tried. Besides, you are not dying, not yet."

"Ah sweet lass, sometimes a person has only a limited number of years. I'm nearly eighty-eight and I have no regrets. Well, maybe one or two but on the whole I've lived a full life."

He started coughing and was still struggling to breathe when Raj came in with a cup of steaming tea. Mac managed to drink a sip and then lay back down. Raj and I kept watch through the night and it was early in the morning when I felt Mac tugging on my hand. Raj must have felt it too because he sat up.

Mac's voice was hoarse and soft and we had to bend down to hear what he was saying, "Meena, Raj, can you take me outside? I want to watch the sunrise one more time over my valley."

The Mac of my youth had been big and strong but now he was just a bundle of thin skin and bones and Raj easily lifted him up. I picked up an extra blanket and pillow. I opened the front door and placed the pillow and blanket on a chair.

"Can you bring the chair to the lawn?" Raj asked and I picked up the wooden lounger and placed it on the edge of the manicured lawn. It was still dark outside and the last of the golden stars were fading in the grey sky. The light from the eastern horizon filled the landscape below us.

Raj gently placed Mac in the lawn chair and I draped the blanket over him. It was chilly in the morning air. Raj then dragged two chairs over and we sat on either side of Mac, looking across the valley at the brightening sky which was changing quickly from dark gray to light silver. The silver slowly dissolved into pink and then gold as the sun started its daily journey across the sky. We watched the sun rise, bold and bright, bathing the world in saffron light and warmth.

Mac's voice was low. "Meena, do you remember that line you read to me a long time ago from *Lord of the Rings?*"

Mac had lent me the fantasy novel when I was a teenager and we had often read aloud our favorite passages.

"Oh yes, Mac," I said. "That's when Pippin asks if this was the end and Gandalf replies, End? No, the journey doesn't end here. Death is just another path, one that we all must take. The gray rain-curtain of this world rolls back, and all turns to silver glass and then you see it. What? asks Pippin. White shores, and beyond, a far green country under a swift sunrise."

I finished the quote and we sat in silence. The morning air was warmer now as the sun climbed higher above the horizon, filling the world with a sense of hope and renewal.

"A green country under a swift sunrise," Mac muttered under his breath.

I could barely hear the words and bent down to ask him what he had said but his eyes were closed. His hands were like icicles in mine. I looked up at Raj who shook his head. We sat without speaking for a long time.

"He's gone, Meena," Raj whispered. I didn't say anything. We watched the sun climb higher and I didn't realize I was weeping until Raj leaned over to wipe away my tears.

"Mac's true spirit will never leave this valley, Meena. He'll always be here, in every sunrise and sunset."

EPILOGUE
THREE YEARS LATER

Dusk was well on its way and the valley was encased in violet shadows. The green manicured lawns behind me seemed to have absorbed the last of the evening light. Day was over and night was falling rapidly. I was looking forward to our big day tomorrow when Mac's Tea Oasis or *MTO* would open for business. I had just stopped by Mac's house to take care of some last minute details. Raj and I had been busy renovating Mac's bungalow into a Scottish style lodge with a tea bar and lounge. The library was dedicated to Mac and had been transformed into a place for cozy gatherings where a guest could order a tea service whether it was Chinese or English. I had perfected the recipes for different kinds of scones to serve with Mac's Scottish tea blends. My current favorite was a cheddar cheese mini scone flecked with fresh herbs and served with my mother's tomato jam. It was perfect with a smoky cup of Scottish tea or even green tea.

"Ah, Meena, there you are." My mother joined me on the lawn. Both of us gazed out over the valley. "You need to come home. Raj will not be happy with me if I let you wander around in the semi-dark."

I wanted to argue but knew it was a losing battle. I was nearly seven months pregnant and everyone, including my husband, treated me like I was made of glass.

"I'm ready to go home," I said. "I was just checking to make sure we had enough tea bowls."

"I'm sure everything will be fine. Raj will be here by mid-morning and can deal with any problems."

Mala, now the cook-in-residence at the tea room, hurried out when she saw us, "Meenakutty, I saw you standing there in the dark and called Ramji to come take you. Little Mother, I'm relieved to see you are here to take this girl home."

When Ramji dropped us off, I saw a welcoming light in the kitchen. The twins were attending a boarding school in Greater Mahagiri and both of them had opted to stay at the school, rather than come home every day. I still couldn't get used to the idea that they were away for the entire school year. The house was too quiet without their constant chatter. I know my mother missed them too. I was glad I was still living at home, keeping my mother company. We had added a whole new section to our house and Raj and I had our own bedroom and living room suite. The sliding glass in our bedroom opened out into the Pooja garden and most nights I went to bed, wrapped in the scent of fresh flowers.

I followed my mother into the kitchen where we found Devi and Muthi working companionably. The kitchen smelled deliciously of garlic broth.

"Is that rasam?" I asked. "I'm starving."

Soon I was settled in front of the hearth with a bowl of rice, rasam and golden ghee. This soothing mixture was my mother's answer to all ailments.

"How are you feeling?" Muthi asked. "Do you want to take a warm bath?"

"I don't have energy for a bath," I said. "I'll just sit here and rest my legs."

Devi noticed that my ankles looked a little swollen.

"Here, let me massage your ankles," she said. She brought out a jar of herbal oil and then proceeded to massage the oil on my aching feet.

I finished the last bite of my rasam and rice and put the bowl down. I sighed and leaned back and closed my eyes. Muthi and my mother were talking in low tones, the hearth was warm against my back and the spicy scents of dinner lingered in the air. I let the sounds and aromas of my mother's kitchen wash over me, bathing me in warmth and comfort. I rubbed my swollen stomach and felt the baby kick and press against my hand, I bent my head low and whispered, "Don't worry, little one, soon you'll be here with all of us in my mother's kitchen."

ACKNOWLEDGMENTS

Writing may be a lonely job but editing and publishing a book is a group effort. I had a huge group of people cheering me on.

Thank you to those of you who read the first drafts of this novel: Ajay Klein, Alan Klein, Alli Klein, Andrea Green Weiss, Jaya Badiga, Julia McMichael, Lynda Callison Reiner-Leith and Scot Adlert. Your comments made for a better book.

Recipe testing is challenging and Cindy Segur and Nidusha Kannan helped with this task.

The manuscript was revised over and over again with help from Marg at Scripta Word Services and Patricia at Powerplay Editing. Any editing errors are mine.

The book was brought to life by Leslie Browning and Homebound Publications. I appreciate all their efforts.

I love all my readers. Thank you for encouraging me to write this sequel.

Last, but not least, a huge THANK YOU to my husband, Alan who has always been my biggest fan.

Check out my website: www.meeraklein.com where you can find my monthly blog and read up on my upcoming writing projects. Find me on Twitter @meeraklein, Facebook meerakleinauthor, and Instagram @all.the.worlds.a.kitchen

Let's keep in touch!
Meera
November 2019

RECIPES

RECIPE INDEX

I cook by instinct and so I rarely measure my ingredients. Even though the recipes in this section reflect my style, I have tried to add measurements so that you can prepare these dishes in your own kitchen. Friends have helped by testing some of these recipes. At the end of the day, just remember this is not a cookbook but rather a novel with recipes. Follow my blog on meeraklein.com to learn more about these recipes and tips on cooking them.

Banana Raita

Beet Sandwiches with Cilantro Pesto

Cilantro Pesto

Carrot Halwa

Chocolate Mousse

Cold White Rice

Cracked wheat pilaf

Ginger Scones

Griddle Cakes with vegetables

Indian Vegetable Sauté

Late Summer Tomato Broth Stew

Lemon Rasam

Mango Salsa

Pulli Curry

Quick Lemon Pickle Recipe

Roasted Veggie lasagna

Saraswathi's Simple Dal Soup

Simple Green Beans

Spicy Stew

Spinach patties

Sweet Potato griddle cake with Mango Salsa

Yogurt with cucumber and herbs

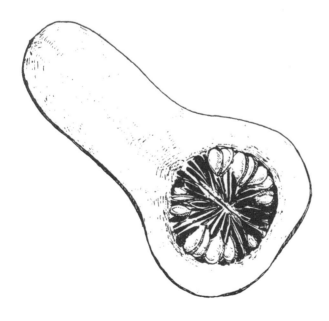

BANANA RAITA

The first time my son tasted Banana Raita it was accompanied with a cracked wheat breakfast dish called Uppma (See Quinoa version), his exact words were, "You Indians sure know how to mix different things to make it all taste really good."

Nothing could be simpler than this dish but the flavors meld together to complement spicy dishes. Other versions include cucumber raita, mango raita, pineapple raita and my favorite, tomato/onion raita. NOTE: All dals available at local South East Asian stores or online.

Ingredients:
1 cup plain yogurt, any type
1 ripe banana, peeled and sliced into small pieces
2 tsp. vegetable oil
1 tsp. black mustard seeds
1 tablespoon lentils: urid, channa or yellow split peas*
1 sprig curry leaf, if available
½ tsp. salt
Black pepper to taste

Preparation: Mix the cut bananas in the yogurt. Add salt and pepper. Set aside. Heat oil in a saucepan and allow the mustard seeds to pop. Immediately add the lentils and curry leaf, if using, fry until golden brown. Add this to the banana yogurt mixture. Mix thoroughly. Serve with Quinoa Uppma, rice or Indian flat bread. Or eat as is for breakfast.

Serves 2

BEET SANDWICHES WITH CILANTRO PESTO

My mother loved beets and was always looking for new ways to prepare this colorful vegetable. She tasted beet and boiled potato sandwiches while living in Mumbai. These are my version of the famous street food. I've omitted the potatoes because I love to use different colored beets. Feel free to add a slice or two of boiled potato.

Ingredients:
2 medium or 3 small beets, scrubbed clean
Water for boiling
1 tablespoon Balsamic Vinegar
2-3 tablespoons olive oil
Salt and cracked pepper

Beets *Preparation:* Place the scrubbed beets in a saucepan and cover them with water. Bring to a boil, reduce heat and simmer until beets are fork-tender, about 10-15 minutes. Drain and set aside to cool. When cool enough to touch, peel and slice them into ¼ inch pieces. Toss the sliced beets in the Balsamic Vinegar, oil, salt and pepper. Set aside to marinate.

Cilantro Pesto: Indians have been making chutney or a version of pesto for centuries. I've added walnuts but you can easily substitute cooked chickpeas if you have a nut allergy.

Ingredients:

1 cup packed fresh cilantro leaves, rinsed and roughly
   chopped, remove large stems
⅓ cup raw walnut bits

1 small onion or shallot, peeled and cut into small pieces,
about ¼ cup
2-3 tsp. lemon juice
3-5 tablespoons water, as needed
½ - 1 fresh green chili (optional)
2-4 tablespoon any kind of vegetable oil
1 tsp. black mustard seeds
1 tablespoon lentils: urid dal, channa dal
or yellow split peas
Salt to taste, scant ¾ tsp and Black pepper to taste

Preparation: Using a food processor or blender, process or blend all the ingredients except oil, mustard seeds and lentils. Taste for salt and lemon. The pesto should be fairly thick and tangy. Heat oil in a sauce pan and add mustard seeds. Wait for the seeds to pop and then immediately add lentils. Fry lentils a couple of minutes until golden brown then add to pesto. Stir thoroughly.

Sandwich Preparation: Four slices toasted whole grain bread or Italian Crusty bread. Spread a generous amount of cilantro pesto on each toasted slice. Arrange beets on top of the pesto. Place the second piece of toast on top of the beets, slice in half and enjoy with sweet ginger tea.

Note: You can add a few fresh Arugula or watercress leaves. Iceberg lettuce adds a pleasant crunch.

CHOCOLATE MOUSSE/ FROSTING

This rich and creamy mousse is our family's go-to frosting. Whether we use it as frosting or eat it as dessert we prefer it to be on the slightly bittersweet side. Feel free to add more sugar to taste. Warning: The mousse tastes so light and airy; you will be tempted to eat it all. This mousse does not have any thickening agent so it will get runny after a day or two and will start to taste like rick chocolate milk. But I've never had any complaints! Keep refrigerated, of course.

Ingredients:
1 pint heavy whipping cream
12 teaspoons unsweetened cocoa
6 teaspoons finely granulated white sugar, or more to taste
1 tsp. vanilla
Fresh berries for garnish

Preparation: Mix cocoa and sugar in a small bowl. Set aside. Whip the cream in a chilled bowl until slightly thick, add vanilla and gradually beat in sugar and cocoa mixture to form a thick pudding-like texture. Don't overbeat if you are serving as a dessert. Spoon about ¼ cup in a small serving cup. Garnish with a few fresh berries.

Serves 8, or one hungry teenager.

Note: For an orange flavored mousse, sweeten with maple syrup and add zest of one organic orange. Chilling the bowl keeps the cream cool while whipping it. Make it vegan by using coconut cream.

COLD WHITE RICE

Cold white rice is considered to be a poor man's lunch but my sister and I have always enjoyed this simple dish. We loved to eat it with bits of raw onion, the tiny red pearl onions, available in Indian markets, which had a mild shallot-like taste. My mother liked her rice with fiery hot pickle.

Ingredients:
1 cup uncooked white rice (Basmati)
1½ cups water
1 tsp. salt
Flaky sea salt
Cold water.

Preparation: Rinse the rice a couple of times in running water and then drain. Bring water and salt to boil and add rinsed rice. Cover and cook for about 15 minutes. Set aside to cool. When cool, add several cups of cold water to completely cover the rice. Allow the rice to soak for several hours or preferably overnight. Drain and sprinkle flaky sea salt. This rice is good with lemon pickle, plain yogurt or sliced raw onions.

Serves 2

GINGER SCONES

My mother was not a baker. Growing up we didn't have an oven so I learned to bake much later in life from some good friends who were excellent teachers and bakers. Adding fresh ginger along with candied ginger gives these scones a double dose of ginger goodness.

Ingredients:
3 cups all-purpose flour
¾ cup sugar
1 tsp. baking soda
½ tsp baking powder
¼ tsp. salt
1 stick or ½ cup unsalted butter, melted and cooled
¾ cup candied ginger, cut into small pieces
1 tablespoon finely grated ginger
Zest from one lemon or orange, preferably organic
¾ cup buttermilk
Baking sugar or castor sugar for topping (optional)

Preparation: Preheat oven to 400 degrees. Line a baking sheet with parchment paper. Combine the flour, sugar, baking powder, baking soda, salt, candied and fresh ginger and citrus zest. Make a hole or depression in this mixture and add melted butter and buttermilk. Turn the moist dough onto a floured board and pat into two circles, each about one inch thick. Cut into 12 wedges. Sprinkle castor sugar on top of the scones and gently press the sugar into the dough. Transfer onto parchment paper and bake about 20 minutes until tops are golden brown.

Serve with tea. Makes 10-12 gingery scones.

GRIDDLE CAKES WITH VEGETABLES

When we want supper in a hurry after a long day of playing and watching soccer, these vegetable cakes hit the spot. If I'm in an indulgent mood, I make each family member a different kind of cake using their favorite vegetable. One son loves corn, another zucchini and my husband loves sweet potato. This is a crowd pleaser.

Ingredients:
1 small onion, diced, about ⅓ cup
1 russet potato, grated, 1 cup packed
¼ cup asparagus diced, or vegetable of your choice
½ tsp. salt
1 tsp. nutritional yeast
Dash black or lemon pepper
2 eggs
¼ cup grated cheese, any kind.
 *I use vegetarian parmesan
2 tablespoons coarse grind cornmeal
2-5 tablespoons fresh herbs, finely chopped.
 *I love cilantro, dill and parsley blend
Oil for greasing the griddle
Optional additions:
1 garlic minced
1 green chili minced
1 tsp. fresh lemon juice

Preparation: Mix all ingredients together, adding optional additions if using. Heat an iron griddle. Brush the griddle with a bit of oil, ghee or butter. Drop a spoonful of the vegetable/egg mixture onto the hot griddle, cook for about 2-3 minutes. Drizzle a small amount of oil on the top of the griddle cake and flip over. Cook 2-3 minutes, so that the cake is thoroughly cooked. Take care not to overheat the griddle which could result in burning the outside of the cake while the inside remains uncooked.

Makes about 6, 5-inch cakes.
Serve with Cilantro Pesto, Yogurt with Cucumber
and Herbs. Some family members like it with Ketchup.

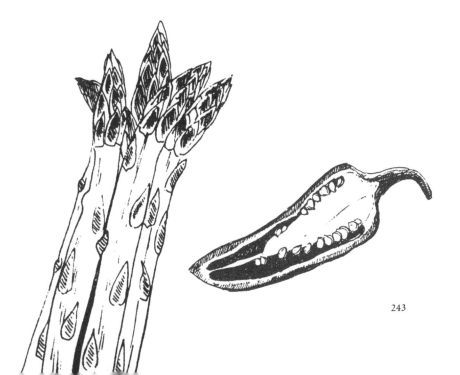

INDIAN VEGETABLE SAUTÉ

Sometimes you just want a simple and easy dish to serve alongside rice or bread. Good all by itself. Or try it with a couple of eggs for brunch.

Ingredients:

2 cups mixed vegetables, chopped into bite size pieces. (Use any of these vegetable combinations: 1 cup shredded cabbage, ½ cup diced carrots, 2 cups shredded spinach, 1 cup diced cauliflower or broccoli, 1 cup diced turnips, 1 cup diced potatoes, 1 cup sliced zucchini, 1 cup fresh or frozen peas)
¼ cup water or as needed (use sparingly)
1 medium red or white onion, sliced thin
1 garlic clove, chopped or ½ tsp hing or asafetida
 *(See Note)
5 tablespoons oil, (olive or ghee)
1 tsp. black mustard seeds
½ tsp fenugreek seeds
½ tsp black cumin seeds (optional)
1½ tsp. turmeric powder
1 tsp. salt
1 red hot chili pepper, optional
Chopped cilantro leaves for garnish
Fresh lime or lemon wedges for serving

Preparation: Heat oil in a pan with a lid. Add mustard seeds and wait for seeds to pop and turn grey. Immediately add onion, the optional hot pepper, seeds and turmeric powder. Sauté until the onions are wilting, a few minutes. Add chopped vegetables and salt. Sauté on high heat until vegetables are tender and slightly charred. This is a quick process and you need to stir the veggies so they don't burn or overcook. Don't add water unless the vegetables need to cook more and are sticking to the pan. Taste for salt. Top with cilantro leaves. Serve with basmati rice, with lemon or lime wedges.

Serves 2-4

Note: Asafetida or hing is a dried form of a resin that has a pungent scent. When fried in oil, its fragrance is like very much like onion or garlic and so makes a good substitute for onions and garlic in a dish. Most south Indian curries call for a pinch of this resin.

LATE SUMMER TOMATO BROTH STEW

Late summer tomatoes, those hanging on after the first cool day in October, seem to be filled with extra flavor and color.

Tomato Lentil Broth
Ingredients:
6 large ripe tomatoes, cut into quarters
1 cup lentils, any type, rinsed.
 *I use red lentils because they cook quickly
A variety of vegetables: A couple of potatoes, yams, an onion, a carrot, a celery stalk, slice of pumpkin, anything you have leftover in the fridge.
Handful fresh herbs, stalks and all
5 cups water
1 tsp. salt
1-inch piece of ginger cut into pieces
1 onion, cut into quarters.
Dash turmeric powder

Preparation: Bring water to boil. Add lentils, all vegetables, salt and turmeric. Simmer for 20-25 minutes. Strain and set aside

Soup Recipe:
Ingredients:
1 medium yellow onion, cut into small pieces
2 garlic cloves, sliced thin
4 tablespoon oil, I use grapeseed oil
1 tsp. black mustard seeds
½ tsp. cumin seeds

2 medium potatoes, washed and cut into chunks, peeling is optional
½ cup green beans cut into 1 inch pieces
1 carrot, cut into rounds
½ cup shredded cabbage
1 tablespoon grated ginger.
1 tsp. salt
Fresh cilantro leaves for garnish

Preparation: Heat oil in a large soup pot. Add mustard seeds and cover the pot. As soon as the seeds pop, add cumin seeds and onions. Sauté for a couple of minutes and then add garlic, and stir. Add all the vegetables, including ginger and salt. Mix well. Add 2 cups of broth and simmer until vegetables are tender. Add another cup or more of broth if the soup is too thick. Garnish with cilantro leaves. Serve with Indian bread or rice.

Makes generous 3 cups of soup.

LEMON RASAM

This tangy soup is a staple in our household. When we want something creamy, I blend everything together for a soothing soup. This is perfect on rice or with Indian rotis.

Ingredients:
½ cup red lentils, rinsed
2-4 cloves garlic, peeled and sliced (not too thin)
1 tsp. fresh ground black pepper (or more to taste)
1 tsp. sea salt
4 tsp. ghee or vegetable oil
1 tsp. black mustard seeds
1 tsp. cumin seeds
1 tsp. turmeric powder
1 tablespoon cumin seed powder
Pinch of hing or asafetida (see note below)
2 cups water
Juice from half lemon, add more as needed
Fresh cilantro leaves for garnish

Preparation: Heat oil in a saucepan with a lid and add mustard seeds. After they pop, immediately add garlic and cumin seeds. Sauté for a couple of minutes, don't let the garlic brown and turn bitter. Add ground spices and salt and allow them to be coated in warm oil. Add water and rinsed lentils. Bring to a boil and then cover and simmer until lentils are tender (about 20-25 minutes). Remove from heat. Add lemon juice, one tablespoon at a time to achieve a tangy flavor. You can serve this with cilantro OR blend the cooled rasam for a smooth and creamy soup.

Garnish with cilantro and serve over rice.
Serves 2

Note: Asafetida or hing is a dried form of a resin that has a pungent scent. When fried in oil, its fragrance is like very much like onion or garlic and so makes a good substitute for onions and garlic in a dish. Most south Indian curries call for a pinch of this resin.

MANGO SALSA

In India, the start of the mango season is a day of celebration. When we were young, my sister and I couldn't wait for try the first mango. This salsa has a south Indian twist, the addition of mustard seeds. Good with any Griddle Cake recipe or corn chips.

Ingredients:
1 ripe mango, peeled and cut into small chunks
1 small white (Vidalia if you can find it) onion, finely diced
2 ripe tomatoes, chopped into small bits
½ to 1 tablespoon red wine or apple cider vinegar or fresh lime juice
1 tsp. salt
1 green chili (optional, but what is salsa without some heat?)
Fresh cilantro leaves for garnish
2-4 tablespoons vegetable oil (I use grapeseed oil)
1 tsp. brown mustard seeds

Preparation: Mix all ingredients together, except oil and mustard seeds, and set aside. Warm oil in a pan with a lid and add seeds. Once seeds pop and turn gray, remove from heat and pour over prepared salsa. Mix well. Serve with Spinach Patties or Griddle Cakes.

Makes a generous cup.

PULLI CURRY

Years ago, when our family visited an aunt in Palghat, Kerala, she immediately set about making this curry. Pulli is a simple dish that is usually served over white rice. My Palghat aunt's version was mouth-burning hot, but it didn't stop me from eating it. In traditional Pulli Curry, no vegetables, except hot peppers, are added. But I like the addition of a few vegetables to give the tart broth some balance and nutrition.

Ingredients:
1 small onion, any color, diced
1 small bell pepper, any color, diced
1 small fresh green chili (optional)
1 large carrot, grated
½ cup shredded cabbage
1-2 tablespoons tamarind paste (See NOTE)
2 cups water
1 tsp. salt
1 tablespoon brown sugar (more to taste)
4 tablespoon vegetable oil
1 tsp. black, mustard seeds
1 tsp. turmeric
½ tsp. fenugreek seeds

Preparation: Heat oil in a large saucepan with lid. Add mustard seeds and cover pan. Once the seeds pop and turn grey, add fenugreek seeds and vegetables. Sauté for a couple of minutes and then add turmeric and salt. Mix thoroughly. Add water and tamarind paste. Bring to a boil. Let the mixture boil for about 10 minutes. Add sugar. The sauce is tangy with an earthy sweet-sour flavor. If the chili is added, it can be quite spicy. Serve over warm rice, brown or white.

Serves 2, generously.

Note: Tamarind concentrate and tamarind paste are the same product. Aunt Patti is a brand sold in local Co-ops and other stores in California. TAMCO is the product found in most Indian and Middle-Eastern grocery stores. The flavor is intense. Start with 1 tablespoon, taste and then add more if needed.

QUICK LEMON PICKLE

One afternoon we had some unexpected guests pop in at lunch time and my mother was horrified to discover she was completely out of pickles! She quickly whipped up these lemon pickles and luncheon was served without any other mishaps. And the family's pickle honor was restored.

Ingredients:
4 Eureka lemons, the type with thick skin,
 preferably organic
4 tablespoons sesame or mustard oil
 *(1 tablespoon of this oil is used to sauté the lemons)
1 tsp. black mustard seeds
1 tsp. each of the following: cayenne pepper, coriander seeds, cumin seeds, fenugreek seeds, whole peppercorns
1½ tsp. salt, kosher is preferred

Preparation: Wash the lemons and pat dry. Heat a large sauce pan; add 1 tablespoon sesame oil and the whole lemons. Gently turn them over so that each side gets browned. Remove from heat and cool. Once the lemons are cool, cut them into small pieces, along with the peel. Remove all seeds and white pith in the middle.

Heat 3 tablespoons of oil in a saucepan with lid and add mustard seeds. Cover the pan and once the seeds pop, add spices and salt. Stir in lemons. Remove from heat. You can store lemon pickle in a clean jar for about 3 days in the refrigerator. Serve with Cold White Rice, even on toast.

Serves 2-4

ROASTED VEGGIE LASAGNA

This dish may seem to have a lot of steps but once the vegetables are cut and roasting, it just takes a few minutes to put it all together. While the vegetables are roasting, grate the cheese and make a tomato sauce, if you wish.

Ingredients:
4 cups assorted vegetables, carrots, broccoli, or cauliflower, chopped in large chunks
1 red onion, cut into thick wedges
1 red pepper, cut into eighths
Olive oil
Salt and fresh pepper
1-3 tablespoons balsamic vinegar
2 cups ricotta cheese
2 eggs
2 cups grated mozzarella cheese, I use a vegetarian variety
½ cup parmesan cheese, I use a vegetarian variety
¼ cup fresh basil, chopped fine
½ cup chopped raw walnuts
3 cups prepared marinara sauce, homemade or jarred
9-10 lasagna noodles, cooked al dente and soak in cold water (see Note)

Preparation: Pre-heat oven to 400 degrees. Toss the cut vegetables with salt, pepper, olive oil and vinegar in a large bowl. Place the vegetables in a single layer on a parchment-lined baking tray. Roast until tender, but not mushy, about 20 minutes. Take the vegetables out of the oven and lower the temperature 350 degrees.

The vegetables can be transferred to the same bowl used to dress them. Allow them to cool to room temperature. Add ricotta cheese, 1½ cups mozzarella cheese, eggs, walnuts, and fresh herbs and mix thoroughly. Place about one-third cup of the marinara sauce on the bottom of a 9x13-inch casserole pan. Place 3 cooked lasagna noodles over the sauce. Layer half of the vegetable cheese mixture on top of the noodles. Drizzle some sauce over the vegetables and then place another three noodles over the vegetables. Layer the rest of the vegetable-cheese mixture over the noodles and top off with the four remaining noodles. Spoon the rest of the sauce over the noodles. Cover tightly and bake for 30 minutes until the sauce is bubbling. After 30 minutes, take off the foil and add the remaining mozzarella cheese and parmesan cheese on top of the casserole. Bake for an additional 5-10 minutes until the cheese is melted. Let the lasagna cook for 15-20 minutes before cutting.

Bakes one casserole which serves 4 people.

Note: I've made this recipe using uncooked noodles and it still works. Just make sure there is plenty of sauce on the bottom and increase the baking time by about 15-20 minutes.

SARASWATHI'S SIMPLE DAL SOUP

Saraswathi is a fictitious character in this book but her tasty dal soup is based on my mother's recipe. In early spring, my mother would come home from the local market with large bunches of tender green onions. She used the entire onion, right down the very tips to make this dal. My sister hated the long strands of onions, but my mother and I loved them. You can leave the onion stems whole or chop them into bits because how you chop the onions does not affect the taste of this dish.

Ingredients:
1 cup lentils (any kind, brown, yellow or red), rinsed
2 cups water
1 bunch green onions, all of the whites
 and most of the greens
1 tbsp. ginger, minced
3 tbsp. ghee
1 tsp. black mustard seeds
1 tsp. cumin seeds
1½ tsp. cumin powder
1 tsp. ground turmeric powder
2 tsp. garam masala (you can substitute curry powder)
1 tsp. salt
Fresh ground black pepper to taste
Lemon wedges and fresh springs of cilantro
Plain yogurt for topping

Preparation: Heat the ghee in a sauce pan with a lid, add mustard seeds and cover the pan. Once the seeds pop, add green onions, spices and garlic. Sauté for just a few seconds and then add water, salt and rinsed lentils. Bring to a boil and then simmer until lentils are tender; about 20 minutes. Stir in black pepper and garnish with cilantro sprigs. Serve with lemon wedges and plain yogurt on the side.

Serves 2. Eat with plain rice or Indian-style bread.

SIMPLE GREEN BEANS

My mother loved cooking vegetables in sesame oil and garlic. Her two favorite ingredients are combined here with green beans for a simple but satisfying dish. She used long Chinese beans for this dish. This may seem like a lot of garlic but you'll be surprised how mellow their flavor is in the finished dish. Feel free to cut back to 4 or 5 cloves of garlic, if you wish.

Ingredients:
2 cups fresh green beans, cut into 2-inch pieces
2-4 tablespoons sesame oil
1 tsp. black mustard seeds
8 cloves garlic, sliced thin
1 tsp. salt
Freshly ground pepper

Preparation: Heat oil in a pan with a lid and add mustard seeds. Cover the pan and as soon as the seeds pop, immediately add the cut beans. Cook on medium high heat for about 5 minutes, stirring frequently. Add salt and garlic. Continue to cook until the beans are tender and slightly charred. Add a generous grinding of freshly ground pepper. These beans make great finger food or wrapped up in a warm roti or tortilla with a bit of hummus.

Serves 2.

SPICY STEW

When root vegetables are available, this stew is a perfect on warm Basmati rice. The chilies and ginger give it a bit of heat; feel free to use all or none of the recommended amount. Chilies in the winter are much milder. I like to squeeze a generous amount of lemon juice over my bowl of stew.

Ingredients:
3 cups root vegetables (potatoes, yams, turnips) , cut into large chunks. Use a combination of these vegetables or just one variety
2 cups cold water
1 medium onion, diced
1 bell pepper, any color, diced
1-inch ginger root, chopped fine or grated
4 tomatoes, chopped into small pieces
½ cup corn kernels (fresh or frozen)
1 cup cooked beans, any type kidney, pinto, black.
*Canned beans are okay
1 tsp. fresh grated turmeric root, if available, or powder
1 tablespoon coriander powder
1 tsp. cumin powder
1 tsp. cayenne pepper
1-3 fresh green chilies, diced (to taste)
2 tsp. salt or to taste
4 tablespoon vegetable oil, like coconut oil
1 tsp. black mustard seeds
Garnish with lemon slices and fresh cilantro sprigs

Preparation: Heat oil in a large pot, add mustard seeds. Cover the pan and once the seeds pop, immediately add onions, pepper, and ginger. Sauté for about 5 minutes. Add turmeric and rest of spices. Let it warm for one minute and then add tomatoes, 1 cup of water, the root vegetables, chopped chilies and salt. Let the mixture come to a boil. Lower heat and simmer for 10-15 minutes until vegetables are tender. Add beans and corn. Simmer for 5 minutes. Add more water if the stew is too thick. Taste for salt. Garnish with lemon slices and cilantro sprigs.

Serves 2-4

SPINACH PATTIES

We love these flavorful little cakes. These cakes are an easy way to get more vegetables into your diet. Serve with ketchup, bottled hot sauce, Cilantro Pesto or Mango Salsa.

Ingredients:
2 cups finely chopped fresh spinach leaves
1 russet potato, grated (peeling is optional)
1 egg
¼ cup feta cheese, *I use a vegetarian variety
Fresh pepper to taste
Pinch of salt, *I use Himalayan Pink salt
2 tablespoons fresh herbs, finely chopped
Butter or vegetable oil for griddle, *I use grapeseed oil

Preparation: Mix all ingredients together. Heat a griddle and when warm, add a dab of butter or oil. Spoon a generous ¼ cup of vegetable mixture onto the hot griddle. Cook for 2 minutes and then flip over and cook an additional 2 minutes. As the griddle heats up, be careful not burn the cakes.

Makes about 4 cakes.

SWEET POTATO GRIDDLE CAKES

This vegan version has a savory taste. For a spicier version, add a generous dash of red pepper flakes. Try these with fresh asparagus for a delightful springtime treat.

Ingredients:
1 large sweet potato, grated (you can use yam)
1 flax egg (1 tablespoon ground flax meal mixed with 3 tablespoons water and left to sit for 15 minutes)
2 tablespoons chickpea flour
½ tsp. salt
½ onion, grated or chopped fine
2 tablespoons fresh herbs, parsley, thyme or cilantro
Generous pinch red pepper flakes, optional
Oil for griddle (use ghee, coconut oil or butter)

Preparation: Mix all ingredients together. Heat a griddle and add a dab of ghee or coconut oil. Pour about ¼ cup of sweet potato mixture onto the hot griddle. Cook each side for 2 minutes, making sure the cakes don't burn.

Serve with Mango Salsa.
Makes 4 cakes.

UPPMA (OOPMA) OR QUINOA BREAKFAST PILAF

Urid dal is a white lentil available in Indian stores or online.

Ingredients:
3 tablespoons ghee
1 teaspoon black mustard seeds
1 tablespoon urid dal (optional)
½ cup onion, minced
1 green chili pepper, seeded and minced
¼ cup diced bell pepper, any color
1 tablespoon grated ginger root
1 teaspoon turmeric powder
1½ teaspoons salt
1 cup quinoa, rinsed and cooked in 1½ cups water
  (it will take about 15 minutes)
1½ cups chopped seasonal vegetables
  (potatoes, carrots, green beans, asparagus or peas)
¼ cup water
1 to 3 tablespoons lemon juice
¼ cup toasted cashews
minced cilantro for garnish

Preparation: Heat ghee in a heavy saucepan with a lid. When the ghee is warm, add mustard seeds. Once they stop popping, immediately add urid dal, if using. Let dal brown slightly, and then add chopped onion. Stir for about a minute. Add green chili, bell pepper and ginger, and sauté an additional minute or two. Add chopped vegetables and turmeric. Stir vegetables to coat with ghee.

Add water and salt and cook vegetables until they are tender-crisp. Add cooked quinoa to the vegetables. Fold the grain gently into the cooked vegetables until everything is a uniform golden color. Stir in lemon juice, one tablespoon at a time. The dish should be pleasantly tart. Garnish with toasted nuts and chopped cilantro.

YOGURT WITH CUCUMBER AND HERBS

This yogurt dish is perfect in summer, Cool with a pleasing crunch from the cucumbers. We use this as a topping on any of the Griddle Cake or Spinach Patties recipes. This is a very forgiving recipe and the amount is really up to you…how much do you want to make? Make it vegan with coconut yogurt and generous squeeze of fresh lemon juice.

Ingredients:
Plain yogurt, any kind (flexible from 1 to 3 cups)
½ cup or more (again flexible) chopped mint leaves
½ cup or more chopped cilantro leaves
1 cucumber, peeled and diced
Salt and pepper to taste
Fresh lime or lemon juice.
 *I use a generous amount if the yogurt is not very tart.

Preparation: Mix all ingredients together, taste for salt and add more if necessary.

Makes 1-3 cups.

ABOUT THE AUTHOR

Meera Ekkanath Klein has combined her love of cooking and story-telling in her latest book *Seeing Ceremony*, a sequel to the award-winning *My Mother's Kitchen: A Novel with Recipes* (Homebound Publications 2014). When she is not in the kitchen or at her computer, she can be found picking out the freshest produce and ripest fruit at the local Farmers' Market.

Klein's short stories and poems have been published in online and print magazines and she is a reviewer for the *New York Journal of Book*. She lives in Davis, CA with her husband and has two grown sons.